Praise for

★ "Heart-racing . . . [a] taut and gritty read." —*Booklist*, **starred review**

★ "Charles's heartbreaking novel in verse shows the harsh realities of the music industry." —*School Library Journal*, **starred review**

"Catapults [readers] toward a breathless, satisfying conclusion."
—*The Horn Book*

"Highly-anticipated . . . Groundbreaking." —*Entertainment Weekly*

"One of those books that when you finish, you stare at it for a little bit and need a moment before you can do other things—it is that good."
—*BuzzFeed*

"*Muted* blends the music of beautiful poetry with a powerful and relevant message. A stunning book." —**Margarita Engle, Newbery Honor– winning author of** *The Surrender Tree* **and Young People's Poet Laureate Emeritus**

"A captivating and unflinching view into the dark corners of the music industry where souls are crushed in the silence between songs."
—**Lamar Giles, author of** *Spin* **and** *Not So Pure* **and** *Simple*

"An intense ride that unfolds lyrically, *Muted* is thrumming with emotion, tension and, most of all, heart. A heart-pounding page-turner, from start to finish." —**Debbie Rigaud,** *New York Times* **bestselling author of** *Truly Madly Royally* **and co-author of the Hope series**

"Mesmerizing! Raw and honest, Charles captures the voice of a bright young star trapped between a dream and a nightmare in this devastatingly beautiful novel-in-verse—a page-turning lyrical journey!"
—**Kim Johnson, bestselling author of** *This Is My America*

MUTED

TAMI CHARLES

SCHOLASTIC INC.

Readers should be aware that this book explores issues including
abuse, eating disorders, divorce, manipulation, and rape.

Copyright © 2021 by Tami Charles

This book was originally published in hardcover by Scholastic Press in 2021.

All rights reserved. Published by Scholastic Press, an imprint of Scholastic Inc., *Publishers since 1920.*
SCHOLASTIC and associated logos are trademarks and/or registered trademarks of Scholastic Inc.

The publisher does not have any control over and does not assume any responsibility for author
or third-party websites or their content.

No part of this publication may be reproduced, stored in a retrieval system, or transmitted in any
form or by any means, electronic, mechanical, photocopying, recording, or otherwise, without written
permission of the publisher. For information regarding permission, write to Scholastic Inc., Attention:
Permissions Department, 557 Broadway, New York, NY 10012.

This book is a work of fiction. Names, characters, places, and incidents are either the product of the
author's imagination or are used fictitiously, and any resemblance to actual persons, living or dead,
business establishments, events, or locales is entirely coincidental.

ISBN 978-1-338-67354-8

10 9 8 7 6 5 4 3 2 1   22 23 24 25 26

Printed in the U.S.A.   40

This edition first printing 2022

Book design by Maeve Norton

TO EVERY ARTIST, EVERYWHERE:
MAY YOUR GIFTS ALWAYS BE HEARD,
LOUD AND CLEAR

You know you're VIP

when you roll up to the airport

with a pilot at your side.

Papi, you sure know

how to make a girl feel special.

PART ONE: CHECK-IN

Monday, December 23
Atlanta International Airport
Time: 8:13 a.m.
Destination: Home

are the worst—
'specially during holidays.
But that's not the case for us,
right, Captain Lafleur?

We hustle past the bustle,
sight unseen,
straight to the holding room,
where we'll wait . . . and wait some more,
before being escorted to the plane . . . first.

Pilot perks.
Also: *boss moves!*

This leaves plenty of time
—one hour, forty-four minutes—
for me to explain how it all went down.
I'm gonna say some stuff
you ain't gonna like.
But you've done some stuff
I didn't like either.
So maybe you'll get it.

And I'm sorry, Papi.
For lying. For leaving.
But not for the music.

Even though it took some time
to open my eyes,
I fixed everything, you'll see.
I muted the monster once and for all.

And now . . .
I get to go home.
With you.
Just like you, and Gwen,
and Ma wanted.

But first, I gotta start
from the beginning.

Inside the great white tent
in the community center parking lot,
an emcee tapped and screeched
into the microphone . . .

        "Singing India Arie's
        'Beautiful Surprise,'
        give it up for our next
        Corn Festival talent finalists . . .
        Angelic Voices!"

           Slow claps simmered
           from the small audience
           as three brown girls
           took their place in the spotlight.

Fingers plucked F#m chords
three voices, three harmonies
powered through verse and chorus,
as onlookers looked on,
   and over,
      and *at*
anything else
but the magic unfolding on the stage.

        It wasn't the first time
        we sang and dreamed
        and wished upon a star,
        every wish, every prayer unanswered.

But for me,
I longed for the day
when hustle
turned to gold.
Show it to my family.
Show them who I really am.

        That night, as we celebrated our win
        —fifty bucks and a bushel of corn—
        three amigas lay on a blanket
        in the grassy meadow of Shohola Falls.

"We *rich* rich now, y'all!"
I fanned my sweaty face
with my cut . . . a whole seventeen dollars.

        "Even Black Jesus knows
        that ain't enough to do enough."
        Shak half laughed, half groaned.

And she and I high-fived
our measly-ass thirty-four dollars
beneath a silver moon.

"I'm so done with
this small-time mierda,"
Dali cursed at the blue-gray skies.
"We need a stroke of luck.
Like . . . if y'all could sing for anyone
in the universe, who would it be?"

                              "Kirk Franklin." Shak didn't hesitate.

"Queen Yeli, J. Lo, but most of all . . ."

                              Dali and I locked eyes and belted
                              "Sean 'Mercury' Ellis!!!" in perfect harmony.
                              We'd been stanning homeboy since third grade.

                              "The King of R&B?
                              Wouldn't that be something?" Shak smiled.

And on that night,
three brown girls,
three heartbeats colliding,
laughed and laughed
at that dumbass dream.

                    But as the sky grew darker,
                    the stars undressed themselves,
                and the universe whispered ever-so-softly,

Some wishes are granted
only to the bold . . .

YOU DON'T WANT TO MISS THIS!
Sean "Mercury" Ellis at the Prudential Center in Newark, NJ!
Grammy Award winner, hit maker, pop-R&B superstar!
You comin' or nah?
It's going down Friday, June 14 at 7 p.m.!

Top fan comments:

denverlee01: Calling @dalisaybabe @ballershak, behold . . . A SIGN!

Samiam24: #nah Merc is #sketchyAF #ImGood

Cutierock14: We bow down to #MercEllis all day, errrday!

dalisaybabe: Damn @denverlee01, what kinda brujería did you do? You literally conjured this man up! Right @ballershak?

ballershak: Word. Black Jesus came through on the prayer front! Hallelujerrr! This is gonna be fun!

ANGELIC VOICES . . .

lyrically known as *Whew, those girls can SAAANG,*
locally known as *But, who really gives a damn?*

                Talent dripped through our pores,
                dreams of fame as real
                as starlight,
                but none of it mattered in
                that town,
                        that school,
                                those mountains,
                                          my family.

In Shohola,
nobody won Grammys
    or Billboards
        or VMAs.
That's why soon as I saw
that my *favorite artist of all time*
was gonna be just two hours away,
it was obvious this was meant to be,
so my goals were hella clear:
Be bold. Get seen. Be heard.
This was our chance.
How'd I know?
Because the universe told me so.

Last day of junior year
and Mr. Andrade had the NERVE
to be at the board . . . teaching!

Dead smack in the middle of
THE most boring discussion
about . . .

"What was he saying again, Shak?"
Shak started to tell me,
always the good girl I'd never be.

> But I didn't hear a damn thing,
> cuz right on time
> Dali appeared outside
> the science lab door.

Pretty as an angel,
a smile like the devil himself,
no one ever suspects Dali.

Left eye winking,
lips puckered up,
Dali mouthed, *"It's go time, muchachas!"*

But before we could get a word in—
                    RIIIIIIIIING!!!

Fire alarms blazed,
crowds gathered,
    feet scattered

students
    teachers
            principals
huddled outside
in beautiful
utter chaos . . .
a perfect melody
in the key of
distRactioN.

OPERATION BOUNCE

was in full effect!

Sunroof open,
   AC on full blast
       school clothes tossed
          an in-the-car makeover
of epic proportions
for two, not three:
lip gloss
midriffs
cutoffs

For them . . . not me.

Wasn't catching my stomach
hanging out like that

I dressed myself
in the usual:

too-big jeans,
too-big tee,

chest
skin
island hips
dipped invisibly

Yeah, my body was big
but my voice was even **bigger**.

All I had to do was get to the concert
to prove my point.

JUNE 14, 10:09 A.M.

Ma: DENNY, I GOT A FIRE DRILL ALERT FROM YOUR SCHOOL.

Me: It's over now. Headed to calculus. Then hanging out at the Falls. Dali's after. I'm sleeping over, k?

Ma: HANGING OUT? GWEN WOULD BE DOING SOMETHING MORE PRODUCTIVE. LIKE FINDING A SUMMER JOB!

Me: It's the last day of school, Ma.

Ma: YOU CALL ME AND CHECK IN, OK? PICKING UP ANOTHER SHIFT IN THE ER. PAPI COMES HOME TOMORROW MORNING. DON'T BE LATE.

Me: Turn the caps lock off.

Ma: HUH?

Me: Never mind. See you in the morning.

Ma: BRIGHT AND EARLY FOR PAPI. DON'T TEXT AND DRIVE!!!

Me: K, Ma. Got it.

turned the music up,
let the sound
drown the anxiety rising
bone-to-skin,
laughed,
and sang
in the key of
IDGAF!
Because right then,
right there
I had zero fucs to give.

Not when . . .
summers were made for music.

(not annoying parents)
Mini concerts in the park,
jam sessions in the basement,
hitting up the Apple Valley on Route 6,
to enter the talent contest,
where we'd sing our hearts out,
and pray to win that hundred dollars.
Not each though—
that was a three-way split.

Not enough to do enough,
Shak would say.
But every summer,
we did that (& more) anyway.

Hoping, praying, dreaming
of seeing a talent scout
a record exec,
or get THIS . . .
our *parents* in the crowd.
But I *we* were never enough, I guess.

That's why I had to
make it happen,
nervous as I was.

So we sped off in my Honda Civic,
three tickets in hand,
didn't care 'bout those nosebleed seats,
'cause I had a plan.

And there I was
driving-driving-driving,
while Shak and Dali sang the roof off
as I begged the universe
to make my wish come true.

Because deep down I knew
that moment
that highway
that summer was made
just for me.

(us)

KNOW WHAT ELSE

summers were made for?
Dreams.
Intergalactic,
out-of-this-world,
       to   M
    me   E
fly   R
                         C
                            U
                            R
                               Y

and back
kinda dreams.

SHIT SHAK SAID

"What if our folks find out we dipped off?"
"What if we get lost?"
"What if . . ."
        "What if . . ."
                "What if . . ."

Songs in the key of doubt,
by Shakira Brown

SHIT DALI SAID

"Do you think this lip stain makes me look older?"
        "Do you think my booty looks good in these shorts?"
                "Do you?"

A lullaby in the key of diva,
by Dalisay Gómez

ACTUALLY . . .

Dali's ass looked perfect
in those jeans,
and I woulda told her that . . .
had Shak not been around.

                                          But!!!

. . . that wasn't the point.
The point was
brains outweighed beauty,
which meant
my plan was
absolutely,
positively,
g-e-n-i-u-s . . .
        right?
(of course!)

REASONS WHY I'M SMART (HEAR THAT, MA?):

Metadata.

All-knowing magic,
hidden in pictures,
that showed me where,
out of all the planets in the universe,
Mercury was positioned.

First, at home in Atlanta.
Concert in Richmond.
Cavs game in Cleveland.
Video shoot in Philly.
And then his final destination:
40.7335° N, -74.1710° W

In other words . . .
25 Lafayette St., Newark, NJ.

His arrival time? 10:17 a.m.
Ours?
Noon-thirty.

REASONS WHY I'M NOT:

Fifty-leven girls
thought to do the same shit.

ARRIVING SIX HOURS EARLY MEANT

fireball in blue sky,
aimed at your body
like lasers.

Heat-hugging,
sweat-building
air,
we inhaled,
exhaled
like fiends searching for our next fix.

Steel double doors ahead,
too far to touch,
barricaded by
girls,
skintight clothes wearing,
lollipop sucking,
video-vixen wannabes.

And me.
In my basic-ass outfit
standing beside
Dali (Miss Universe)
and Shak (legs for days)
 Waiting . . .
          Waiting . . .
                    Waiting . . .

ACCORDING TO INSTAGRAM

Sean "Mercury" Ellis was inside the Prudential.
Mic check done, ready to hit the streets,
grab a bite, before the concert began.

And so we all stood
beneath the sun.

Hope filling up,
fingers crossed that he'd float out,
like Black Jesus,
invite someone, anyone
onto that tour bus parked at the corner.

And I tell you, just like in the movies,
those doors flew open,
pupils combusted.

Stares turned to whispers,
whispers bubbled up
to loud chants.

"Merc is here!"
"Merc is here!"

Hella pissed
'cause I couldn't see nothing.
Just heard the claps echoing,
up, down, and all around
Lafayette like a parade.

Felt the huddle grow tighter.
A stampede of epic proportions
swallowed me, Shak, and Dali
whole.

"Can I get a selfie, Merc?"
voices cried out.

My eyes found a clearing,
zoomed in on a giant
hovering above the crowd.
Security.

Big head stacked on big shoulders,
stacked on even bigger arms,
swatting video thots

like gnats in summer.

I grabbed hold of Shak and Dali,
forced our bodies away from the crowd,
inched closer toward the tour bus.
"It's no use," Dali said.

But I didn't *hear her* hear her
because my eyes studied
the sea of red-bottom shoes
and Timberland boots,
and finally,
I saw the only pair that mattered—
diamond encrusted Air Force 1s.

"He's coming this way. Shak, connect the speaker!
Pull up the track!" I yelled.
And so began Mrs. Doubtfire with the questions.
"Right here? Right now? On the street?"
I snatched my phone from her,
clicked play,
and let that C minor 7th chord
do what it do.

                              And by do,
I mean SAAAAAAAAAAAAANG!

Dali came in with that
soprano note,
high enough to crack a hole
in the sky.

Me and Shak
swerved in beneath her,
the perfect alto-tenor blend.

If music were a color,
ours woulda been blue-red-green
ocean meets fire meets earth,
and I'm not just saying that
'cause those were my lyrics,
my chords, my literal heartbeat . . . in a beat.
I say it because
the minute we unleashed our voices,
noise canceled,
Air Force 1s emerged,
each diamond
bringing more sunshine with it.

Sean "Mercury" Ellis.
Shades slid
to the tip of his nose.
Gray eyes sparkling
beneath the midday sun.
Homeboy was snapping,
swerving,
grooving to "Shoot Your Shot,"
our song—
my song.

Time stood still as
verse blended into chorus,
into the final,
belting, universe-breaking
note.

Applause, thunderously loud.

Eyes upon eyes
stared us down.
But there was only one set I cared about.

"That was dope," Merc said. "Y'all wrote that?"

        "Denver did." Dali giggled,
        then covered her braces
        with her left hand.

There was no time to be shy,
not when the chance to fly
was right in our faces.

        "We're Angelic Voices,
        an R&B group, from PA.
        Looking to score a record deal."
I handed Merc the business card I printed at home . . .

        like a freaking BOSS!

Whispers from the crowd spread like disease.
*"Ain't getting no record deal looking like that.
'Specially McThickums."*

But I didn't *hear them* hear them,
'cause I was too busy
breathing in the same air as Merc.

He leaned in and I knew what was coming next:
"Yooooo, what's up with your eyes?"

Same reaction I get
whenever someone
meets me for the first time.

Always starts with
a stare,
a lean,
a question
(or three).

And for me,
an answer that I
spent the past seventeen
years rehearsing
down to the last word . . .

Heterochromia

As in:
two eyes
two different colors
one blue
one brown
part ocean
part earth
made of both.

As in:
a genetic mutation
the crashing of
two genes
—a miraculous disaster in the making—

No, I don't have a white parent!
(Even though that blue eye came
from Ma's German granddaddy.)
I'm Black mixed with Black mixed with magic.
And no, I ain't wearing contacts!

So, LAWD HAVE MERCY
can we get back to the discussion at hand, sir?!?

(I didn't quite say all that tho.)

"Angelic Voices, huh?
That's real cute," Merc said.
"So are those eyes of yours.
Good luck with the songwriting, baby gurl."

He. Called. Me. Baby.

Security stepped forward,
side-swatting us
like gnats in summer,
while Sean "Mercury" Ellis,
wrapped in a trio of video thots
made his way onto the bus.

And right there,
on the corner of Lafayette,
I almost emptied myself
of wishing, hoping, dreaming.

               Almost.

IF YOU LOOK IN THE DICTIONARY,

it'll tell you that *almost* means:

Not quite.
Nearing.
Not done yet.

I wasn't done.
Yet.

"Let's just go home," Shak said.

   "Oh, hells no! I spent my last dollar on that ticket," Dali pouted.

"What if those twenty-seven-dollar tickets are fake? What if security kicks us
  out? What if—"

   "We gotta trust in Denver's plan." Dali beamed at me. "I know I do."

I stepped back into the line,
felt Dali's shadow follow behind me.
And then, finally, Shak's.
We'd waited that long.
We weren't going NOWHERE.

SCORCHED SKIN,

backs dripping wet,
phone buzzing,
calls from Ma on repeat,
I clicked IGNORE as
time moved
four o'clock,
    five o'clock,
        six o'clock,
double doors rolled out like red carpets.
Lines swerved,
swayed,
snaked their way through
metal detectors,
steps,
corridors.

A weight pressed down on me.
Stacked, meaty arm-head-shoulder of a man.

                "Y'all the singers from earlier?" he asked.

"Yo, that's dude that was with Merc."
Dali's whispered words floated in the air.

"Yes," I spat out, "Angelic Voices. That's us."

"Follow me, young ladies."

One star,
one wish,
one pause of a beating heart
was all it took for homeboy's words
to drink ~~us~~ *me* in.

Dali and Shak trailing me,
I floated behind him,
hypnotized by a long-ago memory:

Bon bagay ap vini . . . *Good things will come.*

You used to say that
to me as a little girl.
Remember, Papi?
That Haitian Creole,
like a lullaby,
always guided me through

every missed step,
    every fall,
            every off-key
piano or guitar chord.

Do you still say it now?
Even though you no longer
have time to sit next to me at the bench,
hands placed on mine
like angel wings,
together,
flying
through notes,
scales,
symphonies,
Bliss?

Because that's exactly
what that moment felt like.
Bon bagay.
(And more.)

VIP meant
no waiting in lines
no binoculars needed
black leather seats so close to the stage.

                        The curtains opened,
                sparks flew, floor-to-ceiling,
                            smoke gathered,
            but only for a second, because
                            there he was . . .
            thin cord attached to his back,
                descending from the heavens
        till he planted his feet, slid to the front,
            the beat kicked in, and then . . .
                            he winked at me.

            I. LOST. my. shit!
            Screamed till every
            vocal cord ripped to bits

    For two hours, every lyric, every song,
    I pictured myself up there with Sean "Mercury" Ellis,
    Shak, Dali harmonizing at my side,

    I felt Merc's sweat flicker,
    as he danced,
    tickling my skin
    like an afternoon spring rain,

Heard the tenor in his voice,
real and true
—no autotune needed—

      Saw the gleam in those smoky eyes
      as he extended his hand,
      pulling her—not me—up to the stage.

Houselights dimmed,
taking my spirit right with it,
as the spotlight zoomed in,
on the silhouette of them both.

      Hypnotized her with the serenade,
      intense from the first note to the last.
      Fingers locked together like chains,
      until the fog cleared,
      curtains closed,
      concert ended,
      and Merc and Dali folded

into the darkness.

A MAGNIFIED LOOK INTO THE LEFT SIDE OF MY BRAIN:

Why did Merc pick her?
Why not me?
Or Shak?
Or some other random, screaming fan?

> He knew I wrote that song.
> He knew I set up that whole
> street performance.

Was I jealous?
Hella thirsty?
No, of course I wasn't.
That's dumb AF.

> A magnified look into the right:

> > Merc picked Dali because . . . well, look at her.
> > Shak had Merc by a good half a foot . . . in flats.
> > Ain't no way he coulda lifted my ass with one hand like that.
> > Right? (right.)

> Also: WHERE? WERE? THEY?

Seemed like Shak
deflated, too, when Merc pulled
Dali up on that stage,
but a nudge from her
faded that magnifier into oblivion:

"Yo, Denver, your phone is vibrating."

No Caller ID: If you need me, I'm backstage, ya know, just DYING!

Me: Dali? That's you?

No Caller ID: Yeah, Merc's security guard made me use his phone. Merc said for you and Shak to come back here. He put us up front on purpose! Wants to know what other songs we got.

Me: STOP

Me: LYING

No Caller ID: Nope.

Me: !!!!!!

No Caller ID: The security guard's name is Meat. He said go to the right of the stage, follow the path marked with neon arrows and meet him there.

No Caller ID: Also, what the hell kinda name is MEAT?

No Caller ID: Also, I'm deleting these texts now.

Me: LMAO! We'll be right there.

No Caller ID: It's happening, Denver. Just like you said it would.

Me: Olive juice.

No Caller ID: same, olive juice ♡

IF YOU LOOKED IN THE MIRROR

and said *olive juice*,
no sound escaping your lips,
you'd see it almost looked like:
I love you.
  Olive juice.
Those words
  belonged to me and Dali,
and no one else.

A reminder,
a code,
cloaked in
two words
that to others
would mean
absolutely nothing
at all.

"YO, WHAT'D DALI SAY?

Where we gotta go?
Over there?
In the dark?
I don't see nobody waiting.
Why can't security just bring her to us?
Denver?
Denver!
Why you walking so fast?
WAIT FOR ME!"

A ballad in the key of scaredy-cat,
by Shakira Brown

WE FOLLOWED ILLUMINATED ARROWS,

like a yellow brick road
   squeezing,
       pinching,
           holding in
excitement building,
until we came to the end,
to meet Meat
and a young woman,
hair of fire,
face of stone,
propped beside him.
               "We need to pat you down," he said.
               "It's protocol." But he didn't touch us—
               homegirl did that.
Used her hands to explore
arms, legs, the curves of our backs,
while Shak and I stared at each other like . . .
WTF?

"Open your backpack." Meat flashed a light
into my pink fifteen-dollar AliExpress pride 'n' joy.

           Then homegirl started digging:
           fifty-leven gum wrappers, three flash drives,
           two maxi pads, one song journal, till she
           found what she was searching for.
"We'll return your phone later."
Sorry, but it's—"

        Protocol. Yeah, got it.

"You wouldn't believe
how many people try
and take videos of Merc . . .
he ain't a fan of digital footprints."

          All good.
          Those were the cards you're dealt,
          when you're a star, I guessed.
They led us through
winding, dark passages
until we reached an open space, full of light,
food, liquor, music.
And people. Their eyes?
On us.

simmered beneath the beat
as I scanned the crowd
of Groupies'r'Us
spread far and wide,
twerking, dancing, prancing
around the room.

"Where's Dali?" I asked.
Meat's expression?
Blank as hell.

"Ya know. Our friend?" I reminded him.

"And where's Merc? Think I can get a selfie?"
Shak added, cheesy as hell.

Meat towered above us,
arms pretzeled tight.

"Give 'em some time.
Prolly showing her around."

But I didn't *hear him* hear him
because Shak and I stood there,
bombarded by waiters
offering up
    vodka,
        ganja,
            you name it.

And Shak did that goody-two-shoe,
church-girl act that she's good for.
"Ain't we 'bout to sing?" she said,
slapping my hand (and my mind)
back to reality.

Man, listen.
If we were back home,
if I didn't have that long-ass drive,
I woulda hopped on ALL of that
with a quickness.
Dali, too.
Who turns down free vodka?

But . . . Shak was right.
The King of R&B

wanted to hear
my
music.

        So I needed my head in the game.

Meanwhile
the tick-tick-tick of that internal clock
reminded me of two things.
It was time to blow.
Then we had ta go. Fast.

        Felt like
        fifty-leven minutes passed before
        Merc did that
        appear-outta-nowhere-like-Black-Jesus
        thing again,
        gray camcorder in one hand,
        Dali, wrapped in a Gucci zip-up,
        in the other.

                Merc rolled up on
                Shak & me
            like we were old friends
        separated by time and space,
                reunited,
    picking up right where we left off.

"What up, Merc? Dope show!"
Shak tried to play it cool,
but those goose bumps on her arms
said otherwise.

Dali,
eyes propped open,
a tad too glossy and wide,
that typical sun-kissed skin,
flushed two shades down.

A look I'd seen before,
in the quiet moments of us.
And suddenly,
a dull ache
simmered . . .

"You good, girl? Whose jacket is that?"

Dali slipped it off,
handed it to Merc.
"I was shivering."
She giggled. "Ya know, long flight."

Code for: high AF.

"Being onstage prolly got to her." Merc winked.
"Right, Say Say?"

"Who the heck is—"

"Apparently my new nickname,"
Dali cut me off.
"Merc can't pronounce Dalisay
to save his life."
                    She circled her finger
                    in the small of my back,
                    a resurrection of sorts,
                    as I tried to pretend
                    like that nickname and
                    that jacket and
                    the fact she smoked out
                    with the biggest star
                    in the universe
                    didn't bother me one bit.
                    (Spoiler alert: *It did*.)

        "Anyway. Thanks for the hookup," my voice quivered.

"It's cool. Had my dude Meat scope y'all out,
'cause I like what I heard earlier.
Would love to hear more . . .
That's if you have it?"

            "Oh, we got it all right."
I was all business then.
No time to worry about
the nerves cooking up in my gut.
Fixed my eyes on the acoustic guitar,
propped against the leather couch in the corner.

            "May I?" I asked.

"Do your thing, baby gurl."
Merc clicked the record button
on his camcorder.
Which didn't help my nerves.
At. All.
                I begged my trembling fingers
                to find peace,
                but once I strummed the opening G chord
                of my original song "Once in Your Life,"
                the vibrations took control,

I saw Dali's whole spirit change,
felt the unity in the breath
the three of us inhaled,
exhaled as one
before we lost ourselves
in the melody of it all.

For Shak, music was
a choice.
Basketball, honor roll, hella scholarships
tapping at her door.

For Dali, music was
security,
a way to help her family back in Santo Domingo.

But for me, music was
the only option.
Bad grades, no other skills or goals.
I wasn't an athlete like Shak
or a beauty queen like Dali.
After senior year,
there'd be nothing else waiting for me.

Soon as we hit
the final note,
questions
spilled out,
rapid fire.

And it was everything
I ~~wanted~~ needed to hear:
"Where y'all from?
Shohola? Never heard of it.
How soon can y'all meet me in the studio?
Next week?
How old are y'all again? Y'all look fifteen.
Oh, seventeen? Eighteen in August, Denver?

"—Bet. Legal enough.
Let me get your digits.
Y'all drive, right?
Let me drop y'all some coins for the ride back.

"No sense in bringing your parents to the studio.
Don't need nobody killing our vibe!
Here's the address.
Come ready to work.
And, Denver, bring your song book.

The whole damn thing.
Y'all about to be the second coming of Destiny's Child.
Y'all ready to become stars?"

OH, HELL YEAH WE WERE!!!

ON ANY GIVEN NIGHT,

a drive up the Pocono Mountains,
that bend
and wind
and end

in Shohola typically means
a sky full of stars,
white-bright moon to lead the way.

But our ride home was nothing but
a dark, rainy cloud
hovering beneath a moonless sky,

And us,
full of questions (what do we tell our parents?),
       worry (what if he changes his mind?),
            excitement (@!#!&!),
                 and $500 (each) in our pockets,
                      thanks to Merc.

Now *that* was enough to do enough.

                              I texted Ma back
                                   (eventually),
                 but first we had to get the story straight,
                              practiced it on repeat
                              all the way home:
            Sorry, we were making music all night.

                 Slipped into Dali's trailer,
                 just before her mom arrived
                   from work at 2:00 a.m.,
                 scattered popcorn kernels
                      on the floor,
               "forgot" to turn the TV off,
        painted the picture of an epic sleepover.

Three girls sprawled out
on the pullout couch.
Eyes closed,
mine moving wildly underneath
at the thought,
the hope,
the dream
that our lives were about to change.

                 For the better.

As 4:00 a.m. hit,
sleep was still not an option,
especially under the symphony
of Shak's snoring in C sharp.

                    I tossed and turned,
            replaying the memory of the night,
                all the times I prayed
                for a moment like that.
To be seen, *really* seen.

The touch of Dali's hand on my shoulder
electrified me out of my thoughts.
I turned to face her,
praying Shak would remain asleep.

A patch of streetlight
glittered the brown of Dali's eyes,
as we lay there, wordless,
for a moment, our knees like magnets,
the fullness of us
existing only
in shadows and solitude.

"Promise me something," Dali whispered.

                            She laced her fingers
                    through the coils of my hair . . .

            "Anything."

                            And I swear right there
                                her hand
                        could've stayed forever.

"Promise we'll do whatever Merc tells us to.
Because I ain't college material,
not with all them Cs and Ds on my report card.
Only other choice I got
is to help Mami run her business,
and that ain't the life I want.
I need this, Denver. As bad as you."

                                My mouth held
                    the weight of two worlds.
                            One that wished
                    we could exist in the sun.
                    And the other that just . . .
                                    knew.

But all I could muster up was
"I will never let you down."

Me: Yo, big sis!!! What up?

Gwen: Good morning my little Shasou, Denny-wenny! ♡ Sup?

Me: Something amazing happened last night!

Gwen: OMG! You got your first college acceptance letter? 🎉

Me: Too early. But me, Shak & Dali went to a concert.

Gwen: A concert? That's it? Girl, Ma is looking for you! Better hurry dat ass home. Gotta run. Interning at the hospital today. Check ya lata.

Me: Yeah. Lata.

were made for family
in the Lafleur household.
Least that's how Ma wanted it.

Even though
once we moved to Shohola,
you stopped
touchinglovingbreathing
the same air that ~~she~~ *we*
shared, Papi.

Nine years ago, when I was eight,
we left Brooklyn,
like some great Black migration,
new jobs, new life, new school,
same problems.
(Spoiler alert: *me*.)

Back in Brooklyn,
the Lafleurs were inseparable.
Me, Ma, Gwen, and you, Papi.
We had a big family,
tons of friends,
music in every bodega,
every corner,
ya know,
actual civilization.

But then y'all got scared . . .
of them city streets,
of the cost of living.

But the cost of living
was much higher here.
For me.

In those mountains,
with the three of you always gone,
Ma piling on shifts,
you flying round the world,
and Gwen, swallowed up by college,

all I had in Shohola were Shak and Dali.
And music. Always the music.

Saturdays meant
breaking out the bottles
of Fabuloso—lavender-scented,
of course,
because if you didn't use that,
were you even cleaning?

Ma and I would wipe down
every square inch of that
big-for-no-reason house,
propped on two acres of land.

A home that no one
from Brooklyn ever visited,
because gas was too expensive
and *who picks up and
moves to the sticks anyway?*

Still, we cooked and cleaned
so when you walked through that door,
familiarity greeted you like an old friend:

te jenjanm,
the warmth of ginger tea spicing the air,

A sweet, hot bowl of labouyi,
made just the way Gran taught Ma,
and kompa music,
stirring through the walls,
out the windows,

and into the forest
surrounding that faraway place
that *never*
        ever
            felt like

H
O
M
E.

EXCEPT ON JUNE 15,

it didn't go down like that
        because I was late
            because I lied
                and covered it up.
Soon as I walked through the door,
there y'all were,
marinating in the smells,
three bowls of sweet porridge
set at the table,
untouched,
cooled down.
        Faces all scrunched up,
            my final report card in your hand,
                mouths ready to fire off with . . .

            Questions!!!

be
some
earplugs!

Haitian papis be like . . .

"What kind of grades are these?
One C, five Ds, and an F?
A little less music, and a lot more studying . . . like your big sister!!!
How can you be a doctor, lawyer, or engineer like this?"

Black mamas be like . . .

"You sure that's all y'all did was make music?
And why would you wanna sleep
in a trailer when you got all the space in the world here?
Girl, you betta look at me when I'm talkin' to you!"

On the outside I . . .
promised I'd enroll
in online summer school,
and raise that negative one-point-nothing GPA.
I'd put on the mask that said I cared,
covered up the fact I was crumbling
something bad.

But on the inside I was like . . .

IDGAF about going to Dartmouth with Gwen.
Better yet, I ain't going to college. PeriodT.
So just back up off me, okurrr?

I figured y'all would change your minds,
soon as y'all saw what I had cooking.

STILL,

Papi, you had some nerve.
All those years,
teaching me,
molding me,
filling my veins with music,
like a hurricane brewing.

> As if the memory
> of such an act
> was one to be locked away,
> golden key thrown to the fire.

I mean, seriously.
Why did you bless me with this gift,
something that truly made me *me*,
imperfectly perfect outside of Gwen,
only to make it feel like a curse in the end?

> But, I didn't say none of that though.
> I kinda liked having teeth in my mouth.

SUNDAYS

were for goodbyes.
The kind where Ma and I
stood at the edge of the driveway,
after holding you two seconds too long.

Sundays were for watching
the driver slowly roll
down Winding Brook Road,
to take you to the airport.

Sundays were for pilot's hats,
fitted tight, as you took to cobalt skies,
carrying people and their dreams
across oceans, mountains, borders,

until you returned to us
one forever-long ~~week~~ *weeks* later
when we played that same, sad-ass song
on repeat-repeat-repeat.

BUT MA'S SCHEDULE

was no better.
Long hours at the hospital,
because the letters D and R
before her name
meant the old,
the sick,
the new to this world,
almost always
took precedence over
~~us~~. Me.

> She prolly couldn't stand
> the silence of home either.

Which left me alone.
Music to fill the empty spaces.
Ever-revolving trips
to Dali's.

> For years it was like this.

Our parents on the grind,
working far from home
because Shohola equaled
population negative zero,
which equaled no good jobs nearby.

> Exhibit B of why moving made
> no goddamned sense.

Dali's mom,
running her own cleaning business,
retail stores by day,
office buildings till dawn.

> Shak's grandparents,
> leading the megachurch
> up in West New York,
> her own parents deployed
> in two separate lands,
> fighting for freedom
> right here on our own.

> And speaking of freedom . . .

My, oh my,
what was I supposed to do
with all that FREE time
on my hands that summer?

> So maybe some of this
> was y'all's fault, too.
> Maybe?
> (k, maybe not)

01905557486: Good morning, my favorite singer-songwriter. Up for a studio sesh on Wednesday? Talk to your girls and hit a brotha up.

Me: Merc? That's a weird number. Is that you?

01905557486: Sure is, baby gurl. Private phone. Aka paparazzi blocker.

Me: Ha! I get it. We'll be there. 💯

10:09 a.m.

Me: SHUT THE FRONT DOOR!!! Sean "Mercury" Ellis just texted me. He wants to see us Wednesday. Somebody call me an ambulance!

Dali: YASSS! I knew he'd reach out! We in there, y'all!

Shak: Guys, I got basketball camp in Milford that day, Bible study at 5.

Me: And?

Dali: Yo Shak, STOPPPPPPP!

Shak: What if we reschedule?

Me: Pick you up from camp, girl.

Shak: Did you even read what I wrote?

Me: I said what I said.

Dali: PeriodT!

Shak: Grrrrr . . . y'all so aggy! 'Specially you, SAY SAY! lol

WEDNESDAY, JUNE 19

Alicia Keys
wasn't lying
when she crooned
out those lyrics
about New York:

concrete city where dreams were made,
and stars were born.

I felt it all driving.
Me in my songwriter chic—
boho dress, leggings, Converse.

Dali: crop top, cutoffs.
And Shak,
in her sweaty basketball finest.

The three of us,
a visual definition of opposite
brought to life,
harmonizing as
Shohola country roads
transformed into New Jersey highways,
filtered into New York City streets.

We parked in the Hudson lot,
pushed through crowds,
hustled down West 42nd,
skyscrapers kissing summer clouds,
the music of the streets
reminding me of the Brooklyn
that was near, yet still
so far away.

As we landed at the door
of Hitmaker Studios,
I pushed the buzzer for suite 3,
felt Alicia's lyrics
all up and through my bones.
Right then, right there,
there was literally
            nothing
                    I couldn't do.

"Thank you for visiting Merc World Productions.
This is Marissa Avent,
personal assistant for Mr. Ellis.
Please state your name
and purpose."

I cleared my throat.
"Denver Lee Lafleur.
Dalisay Gómez.
Shakira Brown.
Here for a recording session
with Merc."

The door buzzed,
soon as we pushed through the corridor,
I saw her:
pixie cut of fire,
eyes like lasers.

"IDs and phones, please."

Homegirl from the Prudential
stepped from behind thick glass,
collected our stuff,
did that whole-body
search thing again,
under our arms,
down the space between our chests,
over the curves of our backs.

Then finished off with:
"Elevator's on the right, tenth floor,
get your stuff back when the session's over."

REMEMBER

that yogurt commercial
where the girl
with the sun in her hair
and ocean in her eyes,
ate a spoonful of yogurt?

And as soon as she did,
she was suddenly flying up to heaven?
Surrounded by fluffy white clouds,
angelic music,
and the pearly gates opened
and there stood the Man himself,
all grinning and stuff, saying:

Welcome to heaven?
                              Well,
that elevator ride to the tenth floor
was just like that.

With a side of nails
—two sets—
damn near breaking
skin in each of my wrists.
Compliments of Shak and Dali.

                              First
thing we saw were walls.
Long, winding,
covered with
gold albums,
            platinum albums,
                    Grammy Awards,
lined on shelves like soldiers,
pictures of Merc with the best in the industry:
Whitney, Gaga, Celine, Mary J—
I stopped counting after Beyoncé.

                    "I can't believe homegirl took our phones!"
                    Shak threw her braids in a messy bun.

I'd have given anything to capture it all
in more than just a memory.
A permanent reminder that one day,
if we really pushed,
if we really soaked in what Merc had to offer,

we, too, could have all of that.

Maybe more.

Meat stuck his head
out of the final door.
"Right this way, ladies."

Seemed a mile away,
the hall lined with closed doors,
three on each side,
a patch of light trapped beneath.

A beat came on,
vibrating through the space,
sinking down to the concrete floor.
A blend of R&B and hip-hop
and everything that was right in this world.

When we got to The Door,
Merc danced around the room,
camcorder in hand.
Shouted out an *A-YOOOOOOOO!*
clicked record,
soon as he saw us.

> "There's my stars!
> Come bust a move with me."

Dali wasted no time,
twerking all four foot eleven of herself,
hips dropping through each thump of the bass.

I couldn't leave my girl hanging
not when that beat sizzled my skin, too.

But Shak just stood there,
hands locked, half smiling.
Church girls didn't twerk.

> "Check this out, Denver!"
Next words outta Merc's mouth.

"I modified the key for the bridge,
took some of the lyrics of your song,

"Flipped it . . .
Slipped it . . .
Dipped it . . .

55

in D
        O
            P
                E!!!

Tell me what you think . . ."
                            The second Merc
                            opened his mouth,
                    that syrupy-thick voice of his
                        took us on a journey
                            to church,
                            to hell,
                            to Earth
                        and back again . . .

ONCE IN YOUR LIFE

By ~~Denver Lee Lafleur~~
By Sean "Mercury" Ellis

Verse:
~~Have you ever had a dream~~
~~so big, so unreal it didn't seem~~
~~possible for you?~~
~~And you didn't know what to do?~~
~~Today's the day, it's now or never~~
~~You can do whatever~~
~~(ya put your mind to)~~

Verse:
Boy, don't take this wrong
but I been staring all night long
I'm feeling you, do you feel me, too?
'Cause I got something to show you.
It's now or never,
we can do whatever.
(ya body wants to)

Chorus:

~~Pull yourself up off the floor~~
~~Don't cha know you deserve more~~
~~Take a chance~~
~~Life's short, take a stand~~
~~Sometimes you'll lose,~~
~~Sometimes you'll win,~~
~~But in the end~~
~~You'll know you tried for~~
~~Once in your life.~~

Chorus:

Let's bounce up off this dance floor.
Meet me at the back door.
For once in my life, I'll take my chance
Life's short, forget the romance.
Let me take you for a ride.
Give it up,
Live it up,
On the wild side
For once in your life.

K, I KNOW WHAT YOU'RE THINKING, PAPI!!!!

    I. Ki caca sa ye??? (It wasn't garbage, I swear!)
   II. How could I let Merc take *my* song and turn it into a ho anthem?

but . . . BUT . . .

I promise
        the way *he* sang it,
        finding that je ne sais quoi
        it was missing,
            felt like flowers
                sprouting through
                    unruly soil.

MEANWHILE SHAK WAS ALL:

"Why can't we keep the original lyrics?
Denver wrote about dreams and goals . . ."

"And rainbows and frickin' fairy dust?"
Merc cut her off so quick it stung,
and everyone could feel it.
                            I took in a sip of breath,
                            slicing the silence of the room.

"No disrespect, Denver.
The theme? Dope.
The melody? Hot.
I kept all that.
But you guys need an image."

His eyes shifted to Shak.
"Time to drop the church girl act.
'Angelic Voices' ain't gonna crack
the Billboard Hot 100.
But 'Untouched' will . . .
Now, y'all ready to cut this track, or what?"

                        Shak's jaw completely unhinged,
                        lips temporarily frozen in the key of WTF.

Mine, too.
My mouth rejected air,
thoughts, words.

                        One piece of me
                        wanted to scream,
                        That's not how I wrote it!
                        But the other?
                    Well, that part knew *who* knew
                            better.

"Denver," Merc softened his tone,
"being a leader means
making tough decisions. You in?"
                            And right then, Dali touched me.
                            Three fingertips pressed into
                            the deepest curve of my back.
                            The ice to my fire.
Pupils, wide and black,
aimed straight at my own.
Code for *Remember what you promised.*
And so I did it. For her.

ACCORDING TO WEBSTER'S DICTIONARY,

Untouched meant
Un harmed
Un spoiled
Un bothered

                                But according to Merc,
it meant
no one else could
compete with,
match up to
what was given to us
by birthright.

                                And just like that
we had a new sound,
new attitude,
new name.

HEADPHONES

                                    gripped against our ears,
                    like skin on bone.

One mic,
suspended from the ceiling,
walls padded in black foam,
thick glass separated us from Merc.

                        Three girls, excitement building,
                            huddled in a sound booth
                            so drastically different
                            from the fake-ass studio
                        set up in my basement back home.

"I'm so going to hell for this song," Shak whispered.
"Take a number, chica," Dali giggled.

And I wanted to tell them both
to quit it
so I could shake off the nerves,
savor the flavor of the moment.
We made it.
I made it.

                        "Let's go from the top, Denver,"
                            Merc's honey-dipped voice
                        filtered through our headphones.

The opening tick-tick-tick
of the high hats
swirled through the booth,
so loud, so piercing,
scaring the living daylights
outta me.
                        Merc hunched over the sound board,
                            his back pulsing with the beat.

I cleared my throat,
readied my voice for
the opening lyrics:

Boy, don't take this wrong . . .

Ever seen a hound dog
cock his head to the moon
and howl?

Well, that's exactly what I looked like,
sounded like.
Three cuts. Each time.
          WTF was wrong with me?

Merc paused the track
hella quick,
and I knew right there
we were finished
before we even began.

I held back the tears
as he rushed into the booth,
feet like wings.

"Let her try it again!" Dali's voice,
covered in *pleaseMercplease*.
"She's just nervous."

"We all are," Shak added,
wrapping her arms around me tight.

But Merc smiled, soft as dawn,
reached his hand out for mine.

          "Denver, baby gurl,
          let's take a walk."

GRAVITY

disappeared
beneath
my
feet

as we slow-strolled
down the hall.

"I remember my first time recording.
I was a little younger than you."

". . . Bet you didn't mess up as bad as I did just now!"

"Worse." Merc laughed. "A whole hot mess!"

But I couldn't imagine,
not even for a second,
the King of R&B
sounding anything other than
blessed by the gods.

We stopped short
in front of a picture
of the King and Queen herself.

"I miss Whitney terribly."
Merc touched the frame
as if he hoped the image would come to life.

"I never thought there'd be another like her."
But then I met you, Denver."

His words set my lungs ablaze.
"But I'm not like—"

"Denver, you are.
Everything and more.
All you have to do is believe.
And if you do, your girls will, too."

The sweet taste of
hope
lingered on my tongue.

He wrapped his hands
around my bare arms.
I looked down,

saw my flesh swell
between his fingers.

"You see that?
You're strong, Denver."

He called me *strong.*
Not big.
Or thick.
But strong.
I liked that *way* better than pretty.

And something inside me just . . .
bloomed.

Merc led me back to the booth,
where Shak and Dali waited,
eyes swimming with wonder.

"You okay, muchacha?"
Dali patted my shoulders,
elbows,
hands,
Mama Bear style.

"She's ready now, right, Denver?" Merc said.

"Let's do this, bro." I puffed my chest
sky-high, smiled wide as a crescent moon.

Shak squealed and clapped
in that *praise the Lordt* way.

Lightning flared in Merc's feet
as he returned to the control board,
beats ready to launch.

"Now, let's take it from the top."

From the very first note,
Untouched transformed,
artists lulled
beneath a master's spell.

Up-up-up
my voice climbed
past the roof,
beyond summer clouds,
soared to distant planets,

rhythm flowed through my veins—
Shak's and Dali's, too.

I could tell
as verse gave way to chorus
the way our harmonies unfolded,
an audible feast of sorts.

Eyes closed tight,
my mind drifted back
to the place
where this music thing all began . . .

FRESHMAN YEAR

Eighth-period bell on blast
lying low,
back of the class.

Chorus,
better known as,
boring-ass,
bubblegum
wannabe opera
taught by Delaware Valley High's
finest,
Mrs. Billick.

In walked the new kid, two months too late.
Tall,
lanky,
bronze colored,
cornrowed,
four-eyed girl, straight outta Alabama.

>   "You must be Shakira," Mrs. Billick said.
>   "Perhaps you'd be comfortable . . .
>   in the back?"

Code for:
with the only other two brown folks.

Shakira did that southern "Yes, ma'am" thing,
sandwiched herself in the empty seat
between me and Dali.

Mrs. Billick plucked the notes from
My Fair Lady,
asked each student to sing.

"How lovely," she said to everyone,
till she got to us,
and heard the soul in our voices
set fire to the room.

>   "Your sound is quite . . . urban."

Code for: *too big, too Black, too MUCH.*
And from that moment
we gave chorus—and Mrs. Billick—
the middle finger and started our own thing.

STUDIO TIME WITH MERC ENDED WITH

1. A promise

   We'll hook up again after my next show, k?

2. A question

   Y'all ever thought about moving to Atlanta?
   That's the music capital of the world!

3. A request

   Let's keep our arrangement on the low.
   I'll hit y'all up in a couple weeks.

   And finally, the strangest of them all . . .

4. A tape.

   Panasonic
   VHS-C
   tiny holder
   of
   a night
   filled with
   magic,
   music,
   Merc,
   us . . . but . . .
                   "What in the Flintstone
                   hunk-a-junk is this?"
                   Shak laughed, soon as Merc placed it in her hand.

   "I was wondering what the deal was
   with that old-school camcorder."
   I laughed, too, tapping Dali,
   but she didn't crack a smile.

                       "Girls, I don't live my life on the cloud.
                       I keep video archives of all my special moments.
                       Ain't nobody trying to hack a VCR, nah mean?
                       I'm guessing y'all don't have one."

   That made me and Shak
   laugh even harder.
                       Dali snatched that tape outta Shak's hand
                       and handed it back to Merc.

"Can we get a download at least?"
She did that bat-her-lashes,
smile-like-the-devil thing.

Always worked on me, but . . .

"Ah, Say Say, I can't have
my music leaking out.
Not that y'all would play a brotha, but still.
How 'bout this? Since you don't
want the tape, I'll send y'all a sample
of what we recorded to your phones."

I ain't gonna lie,
I wanted my song,
the whole damn thing.
Not some grainy video.

I wanted to roll down the windows
of my Honda Civic,
connect the Bluetooth,
volume hella loud,
and sing "Once in Your Life"
all the way home.

But those were Merc's rules,
so we had to be happy
with the gift we got . . .
all forty-five seconds of it.

A SUCCESSFUL FIRST STUDIO SESSION

called for a celebration
with the finest food
Milford, PA,
had to offer at midnight:

Taco Bell.

We sat in the farthest booth
in the back,
killing a twelve-pack
of greasy-ass
untacos

filling that empty restaurant
with the sounds
of three girls giggling,
reminiscing,
dreaming . . .

"Y'all! We gonna be MAD famous!"
"First thing I'm buying is a house for Mami."
"First thing I'm buying is some
holy water—cuz we ALL gonna
need it after that booty-call
anthem hits the radio!"

Laughter erupted
all up and through
Taco Bell,
followed us
all the way down Route 209,
past Shak's spot in Dingman,
Dali's crib in Trails End,
and around the bend
to my empty, empty
driveway
on Winding Brook Road.

No family within
those walls to share my night with,
even though I wouldn'ta
told y'all jack.

Well, 'cept maybe
one of y'all was worth a shot . . .

1:12 a.m.

The dying art of voice mail . . .

One ring
      Two rings
            Three rings

"You have reached Gwen Lafleur,
resident assistant for the East Wheelock House
at Dartmouth College. I am not available at this time
to take your call. Please leave a detailed message
and I will respond at my earliest convenience.
Have a great day and remember
to always reach for the stars!"

Beep!

"Hey, sis. It's me.
I know it's late.
But I did something tonight,
something real special.
I reached for the stars
and landed somewhere you'd never imagine.
But I wanna tell you about it,
over the phone.
So call me back.
Okay?"

Spoiler alert:
She never ~~did~~ does.

I went to sleep
that night, alone,
windows wide open,
high AF on the music,
on my girls,
on long-ago memories . . .

ODE TO BROOKLYN

Summer, Ten Years Ago

Children skipped up and down
the tree-lined street.
Singing, laughing,
lips stained,
with cherry ices, fresh from the truck,
in hand.

Ma sat on the stoop with Gwen,
hands intertwined
in the thickness of my sister's perfect hair,
scalp glistening with coconut oil,
braids patterned in intricate mazes.

Inside,
summer breeze poured
through open windows

Me and you, Papi,
      seated at the piano bench,
            lost in musical bliss.

Prelude in E Minor by Chopin.

Your ebony fingers
struck keys, black and white,
each chord filling you,
me,
with something that felt,
I don't know . . .
Incurable?

You held the next-to-last chord
long enough to tell
the story behind the song . . .

Trapped in Valldemossa,
island of silent nothingness,
secluded from the capital,
where life was vibrant, poppin'.

Hella lonely,
ink bleeding through
staff on sheet music,

Chopin legit banged out
the saddest song anyone had ever heard.

Remember that dramatic pause,
the one right at the end,
where the silence was
long enough
to fill you with the unshakable fear
that it was over?

Yeah, I didn't get that then—
seven-year-old me.

But after one magical night
in the concrete jungle
with the biggest star in the universe,
I understood it.
All.

BACK HOME,

days passed with no word
from Merc.

Suddenly life in Shohola
morphed into my own
Prelude in E Minor,

a bottomless pit
of nothingness,
as I tried to do right,
keep the parental units
happy.

But all I could do
was wonder . . . *worry.*

Were Merc's promises real,
and if not . . .
what waited for me then?

Days and nights
melted into one another
as we waited to hear from him again.

I spent the mornings,
eyes glued to the screen:

Delaware Valley High's
online summer school.

Tried my best to soak in
every essay,
poem,
play
by every dead white author
I "forgot" to read
in American Lit.

Three lessons a day,
thirty minutes apiece,
followed by a quiz.

I zipped through each,
passed with flying colors.
*Thank you, CliffsNotes,
thank you, Alexa.*

AFTERNOONS

were made for Dali and me.

> She'd show up
> unannounced
> carrying those
> special things
> with her,
> invisibly tucked
> in each pocket.

Two flags.
One white—my favorite.

> The metaphorical
> definition of surrender.

Waved it high,
proud,
with
abandon
> as we melted
> into a rapture
> of *touchinglovingbreathing*

So long as the walls
within
kept the story of us
untold, kept

Away from Shak
who was busy
workingchurchingballing

> And then,
> the other flag.
> Red cloth
> ripped,
> dipped
> in alert.

Only to be raised
when sun bid moon
farewell,
as the sound of Shak's tires
slow-rolled up

my unpaved driveway.
And for as much
as afternoons were bliss
the nights were equally so

Shak
        Dali
                Me

Gathered around
the campfire.

                Three girls
                now known
                lyrically
                as
                Untouched

scatting beneath
navy skies,
guitar in my hand,
D major chords on repeat,
mulling over the question
that loomed above our heads:
                When do we tell our parents?

"I know Nana and Pop are old and
low-key clueless, but I think we gotta say something.
No more sneaking off, ya know?
Let our folks arrange all this for us."

                        "Arrange what, Shak?" I asked.

"Contracts? Lawyers? Don't we need that stuff?"

                "We don't need all that." Dali kept humming,
                soprano sweet.
                "Merc wants us."

"And what if he stops?" Shak's eyes narrowed.

The songs of night blended with our own.
Crickets chirping.
Fire crackling.
Branches swaying.

                "He won't. He knows exactly what he wants
                from each one of us. We just gotta give it to him,"
                Dali said,

the veins in her neck
thick like tree roots.

"What's that supposed to mean?"
My fingers stopped strumming.

"Nothing." Dali refilled her cup with rum,
took a big-ass gulp.

"Oh, come on, *Say Say*!
You know it's
MAD one-hit wonders out there.
All I'm saying is we need a
backup plan if Merc loses interest."

"Let's not give him a reason to," I said,
swallowing my own fear of the what-if.

"Okay, *Whitney*."
Shak raised her hands in surrender.
"You're right, Dali. Merc's obsessed with *Untouched*!"

Shak and Dali dapped
and laughed to the moonless sky.

"Yeah," I whispered softly,
beneath D major chords.
"We'll tell our family . . . when the time is right."

I swear I heard angels,
like a church chorus,
the second we finally got the text.

Merc was in New York,
back from his mini tour.
And the only thing on his mind . . .
was US!

Mannnnnn,
we dipped off
hella quick,
Pocono Mountains
fading into skyscrapers
kissing clouds.

Sick beats waited for
our voices to light up the booth.

And so we did.
We recorded the bridge
and outro for
"Once in Your Life."
And . . .
We. Torched. That. Shit.

"Whew! That's FIYAH!"
Merc screamed
as he replayed the mix.
        I checked my watch.
        We'd been there four hours.
        But it felt like four beats of a heart.

"I'ma need y'all back next Sunday!"
Merc walked us to the exit.

        "No doubt!" Me. Dali. Voices merged.
        "Can we come another day? Like Thursday?
        Nana and Pop will flip if I miss mornin' service."

"Bless your lil' heart."
Merc mocked Shak's southern drawl.
"I'm sure the Lord will understand."
        Then Merc buzzed us out,
        turned his back,
        and kept it moving upstairs.

On the ride home,
we almost tore the roof of my Civic off
interrogating Shak.

"You can't miss ONE day of church?"

"Guys, I've already missed camp
and work *and* church.
I love our singing group,
but I have a lot goin' on."

"So, what are you trying to say
about me and Denver?
We ain't got no life?"

"No! That's not what I meant!
It's just with senior year comin',
and college tours,
the juggle is a struggle, yo!"

"Chill with the college talk." Dali
rolled down the window and
pretended like she was throwing up.

"And I don't know how to say this . . .
but Merc creeps me out a lil'."

Dali snapped her head around,
Exorcist style.
"You two kinds of crazy tonight, chica!"

"Look, I know! But when Meat
escorted me to the bathroom tonight,
one of those hallway doors was cracked open.
And y'all know what I saw?"

"What's that?" I asked.

"Eyes. All veiny and yellow
where the white part should be.
Something was legit starin' at me."

"Ooooooh, maybe it was El Cuco!"
Dali said,

which of course made me
snort-laugh and
almost dive right off the
Lincoln Tunnel.

        "No, Chucky!"
           "No, Freddy Krueger!"

Dali and I
kept going like that
for all of I-287.

But Shak
didn't find it funny.
From my rearview mirror,
I saw her roll her eyes
and coil like a snake in the back seat.
She was quiet
the whole ride home.

Slammed my car door,
raced up the driveway
to her front door,
slammed that one, too.
And then Shak ghosted on us.

H
A
R
D.

Me: Four days, no call, no text? We love you Shak Attack, come back!

Dali: We're sorry. We promise we'll be more careful.

Shak: Glad you guys understand. ♡

Me: Pick you up Sunday at noon, k?

Shak: WOW.

Dali: What you mean wow?

Shak: I'm not going. I told you why.

Me: So you just gonna play us like that?

Crickets.

JULY 6, 3:10 P.M.

01905552702: Sup, baby gurl. See u guys tomorrow?

Me: Merc? That you?

01905552702: In the flesh, well text, ha!

Me: New phone?

01905552702: I keep burners on deck. You know how it is. Gotta switch it up, keep crazy fans and the paparazzi off my back.

Me: Ok. Well, we got a problem. Shak can't miss church.

01905552702: Come anyway. We'll record and then I'm takn y'all somewhere.

Me: Without Shak? But we need her third harmony. And where we going?

01905552702: Just come. Will make it work.

Old-school
1990s R&B
blasting behind
the door
of my room.

Sisters with Voices,
better known as
SWV,
singing sweetly
about all the things
that make one weak.

Like this girl.
Dalisay Gómez,
honey and fire in human form

topknot,
floral sundress,
cherry-stained lips.

An in-the-room makeover
of epic proportions
for our big day with Merc.
I tossed on
my cut-up black jeans,
Converse,
pink AliExpress bag,
scrunched my hair with
Miss Jessie's Pillow Soft Curls.

"You are the epitome
of casual-cute, muchacha."
Dali's fingers laced in mine,
pulled me into her embrace.

I didn't hear the door fly open
only saw the look on her face.

Hands unlocked,
music stopped.

"Ma, what're you doing home?"
Two eyes,
blue as moonstone,
a genetic oxymoron

against
light brown skin.
Her words,
laser hot.
"Denver, let me talk to you."

Dali grabbed her purse,
said *Hello, Mrs. Lafleur,*
and flew her ass straight
down the stairs.

"Where you headed?"

"Girls' date," I chirped, stomach tingling.

"And your third partner in crime?" Ma scanned my room.

"On our way to get her. Sleeping at Dali's."
I lied quick, easy.

"I forgot some files.
I'm headed back to the hospital now.
Pulling a double.
You get to Dali's before midnight . . ."

I took a deep breath,
happy that was all,
but I shoulda known
Ma wasn't done . . .

"And, Denver?
That little thing
you think you're feeling?
It's just a phase."

PHASE /fāz/

(noun)

Definition (according to Webster's):
an aspect or part (as of a problem)
under consideration

Definition (according to Black folk):
temporary disappointment,
human hellbound

Definition (according to Ma):
the waiting
for an awakening,
sharp thrust into reality,
that life is already hard
carrying the weight of the world
in this Black body,
this Black skin . . .

Why make it harder
as a . . :
lesbian?

Definition (according to me):
. . .

Nothing.
This thing wasn't a phase at all.

HITMAKER STUDIOS,

the place where stars
are born

Singing in that booth
without Shak
felt like
a too-small Band-Aid
over a too-big wound.

Two girls,
one new song,
three harmonies,

One press of a button,
vocal magic on a track.

Merc whipped out some Henny
after we were done recording.

"I'll pass," I said.
Needed to be alert for the long drive home.
Shak woulda been hella proud.

Merc's face went all cloudy on me.
If the man had pearls, he woulda clutched
them, too.

But I just hit him with the
"Sorry, bruh" shrug.

Dali swooped her arm to the table,
"I'll take a hit!" gripped the red plastic cup,
gulped the spicy liquid down.

One sip,
two sips,
three sips.

Eyes rolled back,
smile grew wide,
Dali's ass was flying high!

I laughed so hard, I thought
my bladder would burst.
"Where you going?" Merc said.

"Bathroom."

"You gotta ask permission to leave the room, sweetheart."

> I laughed again and headed for the door.
> "You're so funny, Merc."

Meat,
all six foot eight of him,
blocked me at the exit.
"He ain't kidding."

Merc stood up, grabbed hold of my arm.
"I'll take her. Gotta protect my little star, you know."

> And I swear I never felt so special.

Merc waited for me, like a real gentleman,
to come out the bathroom,

slipped his hand around my waist,
fingers pressed in the curve of my hip.

"You feeling all right?" he asked,
lips close enough to brush against my nose.
The smell of his breath, a mix of Henny and heat.

If this were one of those rom-com flicks,
we woulda kissed and
I'da melted right into his arms.

But WTF was I kidding?
I'd feel nothing.
Like, at all.
Not to mention, Merc was like . . .
uncle status,
no matter how fine homeboy was.

> "I'm good," I said.

He loosened his grip,
that whole movie image
just in my head, then gone
as he fist-bumped me
like the homey
I knew him to be.

> And I had to laugh at myself
> for worrying about Shak
> and her stupid heebie-jeebies.

"I got two surprises for y'all.
You ready, lil' sis?"

"Always, bro," I responded.

Right there,
I told myself
I'd always
be ready,
with open arms,
for whatever
homeboy
had up his sleeve.

For better or better.

Surprise #1

I never noticed the single crack
in the concrete floor before that night.
It started from the entrance of the elevator
and zigzagged its way from door to door.

Merc led me and Dali
down the hall,
the light above hissed
flick, flick, flick,
past each door
until we reached the one
near the bathroom

cracked open,
the sinking feeling
that someone *was* watching us.

Merc gripped the knob
and opened it fully.

Lights on full blast.
Three smiling ladies,
staring back at us.

And guess what?
No boogey man.
No creepy eyes!

Instead, there were
racks of clothes
lined against the walls.
Labels for days!

Gucci
      Fendi
           Prada

Mirrored tables
covered in those lights
you see on Broadway shows.

Makeup brushes in hand,
flat irons on deck.

"This is my new singing group, Untouched,"
Merc said to the stylists.

"As you can see,
these youngins need a little help." He winked.
"Give 'em the full treatment."

        Oh yeah, Big Brother Uncle Merc
                status was in full effect!
                'Specially with this next-level hookup!

Dali did that nail-digging-in-my-wrist
thing again.
Only that time, I swear
that pain never felt so good.

ONE HOUR LATER . . .

Every   kink,
every   curl
sizzled   straight

into submission.

Bodies dipped
in a Fendi disguise.

Red-bottoms clicked
against concrete,

letting the whole world know
Untouched had arrived!

Two-thirds at least.

                              Surprise #2

Meat at the wheel,
Merc in the passenger seat,
me, Dali, and Marissa,
sandwiched in the back.

        A ride
        in a Maybach S 650
        was like
        blue paint against navy skies
        matching the pants I wore
        shiny as chrome rims spinning,
        gleaming like stars and city streetlights.

                        Top down,
                  summer heat
              threatening the return
                  of kinky curls,
"Who cares, Denver?"
Dali shook my mane with her hands.
"Let that shit go!"

And I didn't know
if she was talking 'bout
my hair . . . or Shak.
(or-Ma-or-Gwen-or-You!)

                            But it didn't matter.
                  Nothing else did.

Because I was
happily riding
in that car
with #TeamMerc,

blasting Hot 97
singing every lyric
of that old-school Jay Z,
"Big Pimpin',"
with my queen (Dali)
and the KING (Merc)!

The ones who
filled me with hope,
freedom,
and forgetfulness . . .

Like the fact that
Marissa had our phones.

And because of that,
there were texts I didn't see.

JULY 7, 10:32 P.M.

Shak: Merc called me tonight. Told me since I bailed on him, the least I could do is send him a picture . . . in a bikini.

Shak: Like . . . really??? Yo, call me back.

PAPARAZZI:

camera-flashing,
immortal beings
that followed Merc
E
    V
        E
          R
            Y
               W
                  H
                    E
                       R
                          E
                              !

(and I loved ev-uh-ree second of that shit!)

Flashing lights
swallowed Merc whole,
as me, Dali,
Meat, Marissa,
and the rest of
Merc's nameless,
wordless crew
trailed behind him
through the back entrance
of Club LAVO.

Hip-hop thumped,
shaking walls,
bottles crowned
with mini fireworks,
the waitress led us to our own little corner
of the world,
no eyes,
no whispers,
no pointing
as Merc dropped coins
—eleven g's—
like it was nothing.
                    Just us,
                    #TeamMerc,
                    in our own little galaxy.

That night

my brain was
a place
where memories
went to
die.

Wanna know why?

Because what good
was a night of fun
if you could remember
all of it?

Memory morphed

into a repetitious
play of
hide-and-seek,

flashes of my greedy ass
trying every food passed my way.

Every drink color poured
red, brown, clear
equal parts burning
and delicious.

The dance floor
where me and Dali
and Merc and
even tight-faced Marissa let loose.

Hands on shoulders
Waist
Back
Ass

A smiling Dali—damn, she looked so good that night—
that gleam that's stayed
with me since the day we first met.

The clicking of a clock,
vibrations of more texts
I didn't know existed.

MONDAY, JULY 8

3:11 a.m.

Shak: I can't sleep. You're not returning my calls. Something ain't right.

4:28 a.m.

Shak: Y'all leave me with no choice.

8:21 a.m.

Here's what I also didn't remember . . .

How I got back to the studio
and woke up in . . .

that	bed
that	blood
that	sun.

OXYGEN.

I didn't need it.

Sipped in one breath,
held it there,
deep,
      deep,
            deep,
let it swell,
blocked out the noise
of New York City streets
ten floors beneath cracked windows.

Begged my feet,
to find the floor,
knees vs. gravity,
a battle of epic proportions.

Thoughts replaced breath.
Why were my . . .

pants gone,
      shirt off,
         bra still on,
             panties . . . with a pad inside?

                  Fingers gripped on satin sheets,
                cocooned my exposed parts,

Door thrown open,
feet flew beneath
the *buzzzzz* of flickering lights.

Hands frantically
pulled at each door,
locked-locked-locked some more
winding cracks in the concrete floor,
led the way

until I reached the studio,
busted through,
my last piece of strength
dried out

soon after I screamed in F sharp.
Dali caught me

midfall, pulled me close,
sat me on the leather couch.

                            "Tranquila, Denver! Calm down!"
Her fingers navigated
swollen coils of my hair.

"SOMETHING HAPPENED TO ME!"
My voice, soprano-heavy.
                                                            up.
Chills.   up,
          Ran   up,

Heat.
          Descended down,
                                  down,
                                              down . . .
(there.)

Merc, Marissa,
ran in the studio.
Water bottle in his hand,
pill bottle in hers.

          "You okay, baby gurl?"
          Merc touched my forehead,
          skull like thunder rumbling in dark skies.

I pulled away, head spinning,
raised my voice once more.
"Why did I wake up like this?"

          "You drank too much last night, Denver," Marissa said,
          pressing two pills against my dry, cracked lips.

              "And you got your period, like really bad," Dali whispered.

That quiets me . . . freezes me.
Still.

                    Technically, it *was* that time of the month.
                    but . . . BUT never before
                    had my period felt like
                    someone took a drill,
                    pushed it through my insides,
all the way up to my esophagus,
clicked the ON button . . .

And forgot to turn it   O   F   F.

Merc sat on the edge of the couch,
his eyes meeting mine.
But I couldn't look at him,
looking at me . . . looking
like *that*.

But then he grabbed my hand,
warmth pulsing through,
and I did.

"I found you crying, bleeding, drunk as hell.
So I woke Say Say and Marissa up to help."
Merc's eyes turned glossy. *Were those tears?*
"I was so scared for you, baby gurl."

      "You were out of it, muchacha.
      I'm the one who got you undressed.
      (I even put a pad on for you.)"

        Marissa chimed in.
        "And I washed your clothes.
        You got a real one right there, Denver.
        That's a ride-or-die if I ever seen one."

A single tear welled,
swelled in my left eye, ocean blue,
fell down the earth of my cheek,
until it reached the corner of my lips
where it disappeared,
taking the foggy memory
of the night with it.

        "It's nothing to be ashamed of.
        I grew up with four sisters. Trust me. I seen worse.
        Maybe next time a little less turn-up?"

I wanted to believe Merc,
the doubt fading
because of his words
and Marissa's.
But more importantly, Dali's.

        "We gotta get outta here, Denver.
        Give me your keys.
        Go back to the room and change.
        I'll drive us home."

It took me
a second or ten to
ground myself in the space
of the room I slept in.

Bed in the middle,
pillows, comforter
a visual definition of chaos at best.

Equipment lined the walls
microphones,
keyboards,
guitars,
tripod,

and on the floor,
a dusty, old-school
Panasonic camcorder.

I put my clothes on,
as fast as my hands would allow.

A tap at the door.
Marissa.
My phone in her hand.
"Didn't want you to forget this."

Soon as I turned it on,
I saw it.

A new text from Shak.
July 8, 9:13 a.m.

Two words, no explanation:
I'm sorry.

But I didn't even have
the energy to respond.

I SLEPT THE WHOLE RIDE HOME

as Dali navigated
New York City streets
and tree-covered Pocono Mountains,

every now and again
grazing the palm of her hand
against the highways of
my cheek-neck-chest.

"Everything will be fine. You'll see."
Her words, a whispered stitch,
healing, weaving
from toes to follicle
(and hidden parts in between).

Behind closed eyes,
I replayed the night in my head,
Dali's promise of
nothinghappenednothinghappened
on repeat.

Maybe it was the music,
a sample of the new song we recorded
last night that blocked it out,
made it real . . .

A low and slow ballad,
equal parts
Whitney and Mariah.

Just me and Dali,
battling it out,
singing as if
tomorrow the world would end.

It almost hurt to
not hear Shak's
soul-filled tenor on the track.

A broken, empty,
missing piece of the puzzle.

That hollow feeling that
~~something~~
I wasn't right.

On any given day

I could almost always find
the curve of our driveway empty.

Your car eternally parked in the garage
since you were rarely home, Papi.

Ma was always at work
and my black Civic
propped right in front of the red double doors.

That morning though
it wasn't empty.

Four cars
lined up
and I recognized them all.

THE FIRST THING WE SAW

when I unlocked the front door?
Y'all.

Propped on the couch,
equal distances
of personal space
in between.

You.
Ma.
Tía Esme.
Pastor Brown.
Grandma Brown.
Shak.
Shit.

The first thing we heard?

Ma's voice, like a dragon
unleashing fire.
I could always count
on that woman to get the party started.

       "Where have you been?" Arms crossed, left foot tapping.

"At the Falls," I said, "then brunch."
"Walmart after that," Dali added.

       "And last night?"
       Ma's question hovered in the air.

"¡Y dinos la verdad!" Tía Esme's finger pointed straight at Dali.
Boy, when Dali's mom sided with mine,
it was a WRAP!

They wanted the truth?
           Well, the truth about a lie is

once planted,
the seed—
stubborn as the day is long—
will grow
whether you watered it or not.

Red veins piercing through

brown cheeks,
Shak spoke before
Dali or I could get the words out.

                    "When you guys didn't return my texts or calls,
                    I got nervous that something happened to you."

(Something did.)
I wanted to say that,
but the words tasted like lies
on my tongue.

I felt the heat steamroll off Dali
as she leaned forward,
and spat out,
"You're being paranoid!"

I inhaled,
Dali did the opposite.

                  "We went out," I said,
                  legs struggling against gravity.

"With that there famous singer
who asked Shakira for *neked* photos?" Pastor Brown said.

Something about hearing
Shak's grandfather utter the word *naked*
made me want
to fling myself in boiling water.

Dali sucked her teeth.
"Shak, maybe you heard wrong.
Merc wouldn't do that."

                  "Who is this Merc anyway?"
                  Papi, your voice was
                  equal parts mad and oblivious.

"A musician, Papi.
People say he's a genius."
        But you shut me down
        with a wave of the hand
        and that same old eye roll.

Pastor Brown pulled Shak's cell phone
out his blazer pocket,
swiped up, and clicked

P
L
A
Y

"Once in Your Life"
filtered in,
in all of its
bass-thumping
booty-poppin'
thot glory.

If Dali's eyes
were lasers,
Shak woulda been
laid out
flat on the floor.

"TURN THAT DEVIL MUSIC OFF!"
Grandma Brown yelled,
hands clutched on white pearls.

I saw the tears build up
before they fell down Shak's face.
Felt the sting of my own rising, too.

"It's a good thing Shak told us,
lest we never woulda
found out what you girls been hidin' for weeks."

Pastor Brown passed Shak's phone
to Ma, Papi, Tía Esme.

The truth on full display,
a trail of texts
going back to the
very day I plotted this whole
get-famous-or-die-trying
thing.

WHAT GOOD WERE LIPS

if the second I tried
to use them to explain,
you and Ma told me to SHUT UP?

What good were ears

if the only words
that came from your mouths
were sung in the key of:

NO
      CAN'T
           & FORBIDDEN?
What good were tears

if they weren't enough
to stop what came next?

                    Accusations:
        "Your daughters are bad influences
                for our Shakira!"
         And then, a battle
of epic proportions
old-school vs. new-school

      churchgoing, Bible-thumping pastors
              vs.
        three overworked parents

who hadn't seen the inside of a church
since . . .

Dang, when *was* the last time?

glued on wooden floors
a scratch of the throat
followed by a truth bomb,
loud enough to slice through raised voices:

"Dali, Denver, I'm sorry, but
I can't sing with you anymore."

                                    And just like that

Shak's grandparents
rose up from the couch
each hand
locked in hers,

Bibles gripped
firm in the other.

Noses pointed to the heavens,
they ignored our
PleaseShakPlease
sobbing,
          wilting,
                    broken
cries,

And then . . .
they dragged her ass straight out the front door.

Which left
me and Dali with
YOU GUYS.

"I'd like a meeting with this so-called singer.
TUH-DAY!"

Ma didn't care about those tears,
my swollen-up eyes.
Neither did you, Papi.

"That's not how Merc operates.
We need to trust him and his process.
He's the professional after all!"
(NOT Y'ALL!)

I didn't say that last bit though.

Tía Esme came in,
like soft rain
after a violent storm.
"¿Y cuánto saben de este hombre, Dalisay?"

"We know enough that he could change our lives.
We could make albums . . .
have enough money to get a house.
Not live like we do. Get our papers in order.
Bring abuela and Tío here with us."

That last bit shifted Tía Esme's whole spirit.

She hadn't been home in eight years—
We had become her family.
It wasn't that she didn't want to go to Santo Domingo.
It was just the risk of never being allowed back was too great.
And the money?

Never enough to do enough.

THE VERDICT FOR MY CRIMES?

1. Driving privileges temporarily suspended
   (because punishments were still a thing even though I was turning eighteen soon)
2. A promise that me and Dali would never mess up like that again
3. A special meeting with Merc . . . ASAP!

Why?

Because

according to Ma . . .

Teenagers	ain't
got	no
business	doing
business	with
a	grown
ass	MAN
!!!	!!!

It didn't matter
that I, myself,
was almost grown.

Almost.

THAT NIGHT

got no better,
long after Dali
and Tía Esme left.

Behind the closed double doors
of your master suite,
television volume on full blast,
but not enough to mask
the crashing of objects,
name calling,
screaming voices
hungry with blame.

And behind my own,
there simply
weren't enough
scalding showers,
maxi pads,
and Midol
in the world
to empty
that feeling that rose up
inside of me.

All over again.

ONCE UPON A MIDNIGHT,

there lived a girl
racked with pain,
drilled down to the bone
who suddenly felt
her body was no longer her own.

A hymn in the key of what-da-fuq-was-wrong-with-me
by Denver Lee Lafleur

PAIN MANAGEMENT 101:

On the bi-leveled roof
of the big, big house
on Winding Brook Road,
I sat beneath a black sky
full of gleaming stars.

A freshly rolled blunt
placed between my lips,
I made a promise
I'd *never* drink that much again.

I inhaled the earthy, smoky,
herbal essence,
let it glide
                lowwww
                slowwwwww
all up and through
whatever shards of me
the night before left behind.

You didn't see me
on the roof that night, Papi.

Didn't see me seeing you
barrel out the front door,
suitcase trailing behind.

Didn't hear me hearing you
dial the digits,
shift your tone from
stone to honey,
words whisper-soft . . .

I'm on my way.
See you in a few hours.

But I did, Papi.

And I wanted to raise my voice,
scream that I wanted to escape,
get the hell outta Shohola, too.
But most of all,
I wanted to demand
you tell me who,
of all people in the world,

held the power to pull you away
when I needed you most.

Because you knew I was hurting
the second Shak
ripped the music
clean off my skin.

Merc woulda never left me like that.
But you did.

Left me crying,
once again,
as tires rolled
against gravel-covered road.

I cried for you,
up there on the roof,
for me,
for us.

The us we once were,
the us we were slowly
becoming.

JULY 9, 1:03 A.M.

Me: I can't sleep. Hurts so much.

Dali: Me too.

Me: I keep replaying everything in my head. We gotta fix things with Shak.

Dali: Facts. I know just the place we should meet. I'ma text her.

Me: Think she'll come?

Dali: She'd be dumb if she didn't.

SUMMER DAYS

spent at Shohola Falls,
we watched the sun
hover above the mountains,
acoustic guitar in hand,
Shak and Dali harmonizing by my side
as if that waterfall,
and that sun, was made just for us.

Like an earthly gift,
a Magic Eraser of
the bad (like that time me and Dali almost flunked freshman year)
and
the sad (like when Shak's parents got deployed)

Dali and I waited for Shak
to show up at our spot,
so we could apologize,
explain the how, the why,
the what's next???

But as sun turned to moon
and blue skies turned pink,
she never arrived,
even though she promised.
But we sure got that text though:

Guys, I'm done. For real.

THERE'S A SAYING THAT GOES:

We don't lose friends.
We just learn who the real ones are.

And right there up on that rock,
beneath a glowing white moon,
Dali's head nestled in the crest of my shoulder
I realized one thing:

Shak wasn't there from the beginning.
Elementary all the way to high school.

But the girl next to me?
Always was,
always would be.

And that
was not a "phase."
At all.

01905554506: How's my star? Feeling better?

Me: Much better. Sorry I overreacted. I just never got that messed up b4.

01905554506: I woulda lost my shit too if I woke up like dat.

Me: We got some drama going here. Shak said you called and asked her for bikini pics?

01905554506: Nah, chill. I don't get down wit lil girls. We did ask for measurements tho. The wardrobe team needed it.

Me: Ahh, k.

Me: Our parents found out we been sneaking out. And they flipped. Now they wanna meet you.

01905554506: Bet. We'll make it happen. Lunch in the city soon.

Me: Annnnnd Shak dropped out the group.

01905554506: Good.

Me: WHAT?!?

01905554506: Denver, ain't no room for liars n my crew. If there's nuthin else you'll learn 'bout this business, remember this:

Every
body
is
replaceable.

PART TWO: SECURITY

Monday, December 23
Atlanta International Airport
Time: 8:37 a.m.
Destination: Home

I REMEMBER OUR FIRST "FLIGHT" TOGETHER, PAPI.

Five years old,
Teterboro Airport.
                    Me on the left
                              Gwen on the right
                    You nestled in between
                              hands held tight.

Inside the hangar,
our steps toward the Cessna 210
slow, deliberate.

Gwen was afraid to fly,
but I wasn't.
You said I was born with wings.

In the pit,
you placed me on your lap
while Gwen sat,
eyes glued
to the ground below.

You let me press every button
on the control panel,   up!
told me to close my eyes   up,
and picture myself going   up,

Together, we soared above magical, distant lands,
powered through turbulent clouds,
never losing our stride,
not even for a second.

The memory of it all
follows me to this runway now,
in the heart of Atlanta,
as the ramp agent runs
our belongings through security.

And for some reason,
I know I'm safe, Papi.
Just as safe as I was
all those suns ago.

A TEXT FOR SHAK

July 17, 10:34 a.m.

I hate you.
I hate you.
I hate you.
I hate you.
I hate you.
I hate you for leaving us.

I hit the delete button.
Fast.

A text for Shak
(part deux)

July 17, 10:37 a.m.

I miss you.
I miss you.
I miss you.
I miss you.
I miss you.
I miss us.

My fingers tapped
out the words,
erased them
before I clicked send,
before I could tell her
it wasn't supposed to
go down like that.

This text was better instead:

July 17, 10:37 a.m.

I wish you were here.
☹

Because for three years,
we made magic with our voices.
I brought the funk.
Dali brought the sauce.
Shak brought the soul.

And on that day,
it shoulda been the three of us
in the van

with our parents
on the way to New York to meet Merc.
Instead, I spent the whole ride
staring at the two empty seats
in the back row.

One for Shak.
And one for you, Papi.

You gave me the wings of music
and you couldn't even take
ONE day to sit back and watch me fly . . .

A day off

for Ma and Tía Esme
was like
Halley's Comet.
That sacred,
special,
unheard-of event
that only came around
once in a blue moon.

"Reservations, compliments of Mr. Ellis?"
Ma had her Bad & Boujee voice on.
"Right this way, ladies."

The hostess led us
through the ground floor
of the Lobster Club
to a private room
where Merc stood
with a bunch of folks I didn't recognize.
Except Meat and Marissa.

The whole time Dali's mom
was oohing and aahing
at how nice the restaurant was.

But Ma was unbothered,
unimpressed,
untouched.

Meanwhile, Merc was ready to
wine us,
dine us,
feed us
with hope,
promises,
security.

"That's Dr. Lafleur to you,"

Ma said
soon as Merc
dared call her MRS.,
but Ma wasn't done yet.

"Honestly, I never heard of you until recently.
My husband and I don't really listen to, what's
it called? *Trap music?*"

If lightning could have
bolted through the roof
and turned me to ash,
that would've been a good time.

"That's not his only genre, Ma!"
The words slithered between clenched teeth.

But Merc was cool AF in his Armani suit.
Didn't even flinch at Ma's verbal lashing.

"Dr. Lafleur, my artistry is quite versatile.
Not so much, as you call it, trap music."

And then he flashed
                    that fly-me-to-the-moon
                    smile.

All the other times we'd linked up,
it was singing hooks,
tossing back shots,
laughter with no expiration date.

That day?
Merc was all business.

                    "I'm Esmeralda, but please call me Esme."

Merc went to shake Tía's hand,
but instead, she stood on her
tippy-toes, hugged him,
and said,
"Ay, so tall!"

Marissa invited us
to take our seats
at the large table.

                    A team of waiters filed in
                    with our first courses in hand:
                    miso soup and crispy squid.

No sooner than those
plates hit the table,
Ma popped off at the mouth.
"So let's get right to it, shall we?
What thirty-nine-year-old man
records music with teenagers—"

                    "And doesn't talk to
                    their parents first?"
                    Tía Esme came in with her two cents.

                    Merc swallowed before responding.
                    "I assure you, Dr. Lafleur and Ms. Gómez,
                    eh-hem, Esme,

that I was under the impression
everything was copacetic."

"Well, it's not.
They're only seventeen.
Not even done with school."
Typical Ma,
forever bringing up the s-word,
steady forgetting
I was 'bout to be a WHOLE adult!

                    Another round of waiters.
                    Next course?
                    ALL the sushi!

"What are your intentions with our girls?"
        Tía Esme,
        shoulders out,
        back straighter,
        Ma's juju
        rubbing off on her
        like sweet jam on toast.

                    "Oh, I have the best of intentions
                    for their future and their career.
                    This is why I wanted to have a
                    meeting today with you and my whole team."

"Go ahead." Ma separated her chopsticks. "We're listening . . ."

THE TEAM:

Producer
Vocal coach
Music instructor
Security guards
(led by aikido-trained Miguel "Meat" Parker)
Personal assistant (Marissa)
TUTOR

Merc started running down
all their credentials:

Award-winning this . . .
Professionally trained,
college-educated that . . .
Ding! Ding! Ding!
Homeboy said the magic word.

                          Or so I thought!
You'd think that
whole college/tutor bit
would be enough for Ma?
Negative!

"This is all impressive,
and we appreciate the offer,
but how about this?"
                          A compromise . . .
Ma:
"They can record with you
but Esme, myself, or my husband must be there."

Tía Esme:
"Pero not too much. Because I run a business
and I'm working all the time."

Ma:
"We need a proper arrangement . . .
in writing.
Also, come September,
they can't be missing school for this,
because senior year is not a game."

Tía Esme:
"Got that, Señor Mercury?"

"Definitely." Merc flashed that million-dollar grill.
"In fact, I thought you'd bring that up,
which is why I brought these . . ."

Contracts—
the basis
for any business relationship.

"For security—
for you ladies."

Merc had nothing to lose.
He was gonna make bank,
whether we made it big or not.

That contract locked in
every promise he made
to Ma and Tía Esme
and us.
Made every
single
what-if fade into the Milky Way.

Merc made two copies for
Ma and Tía Esme to review.
And when he passed it to Ma,
I moved in close,
chin propped on her shoulder.
She kissed my forehead,
and it was everything I'd hoped for.

Me, Ma
silently reading
the map to my dreams.

Every word,
every letter crashed
into the next.

A black hole, of sorts,
bursting with flashes of starlight . . .

THIS ▮▮▮▮▮▮▮▮▮▮▮▮▮▮▮▮ **AGREEMENT**

▮▮▮▮▮▮▮▮▮▮▮▮▮▮▮▮▮▮▮▮▮▮▮▮▮▮▮

▮▮▮ ARTIST ▮▮▮▮▮▮▮▮▮▮▮▮▮▮▮▮

Demo ▮▮▮▮▮▮▮▮▮▮▮▮▮

▮Nondisclosure ▮▮▮▮▮▮▮▮▮ acceptance ▮▮▮▮▮

▮▮▮▮

Signature: _____

NO ONE IN THE RESTAURANT

                                        could see
                                        my unraveling,
                                        heartbeat bursting
                                        through
                                        shell of skin.

                        No one could see,
                                feel
                        that but me.

Because that contract meant
it was legit,
not just some pipe dream.
A real chance
at a real future.
                        And just like Cardi B,

I was like,
WHERE'S MY PEN?
'Cause I was ready to
sign that joint!
                        Looked like I wasn't

the only one who thought that.
Specs slapped on tight,
Tía Esme
oohed and aahed
through each word,
Dali nestled in her mother's embrace.
"My Dalisay is gonna be a star!"

Next thing I knew,
she whipped out a pen from her purse,
and Ma whispered
something in her ear.
                And in my mind,
                I knew Ma
                was asking to borrow a pen.
Tía Esme signed with a quickness,
asked Merc for a selfie with her and Dali
so she could WhatsApp
this moment to all her peeps
back home.
                        The waiters served up
                        the final course: dessert.

Ma folded up that contract,
tossed it right in her Chanel purse,
and plopped a
green tea mochi in her mouth,
like that contract
        and that moment
                never,
                        ever,
                                mattered.

                        "I gotta talk to my
                        husband and lawyer first."

HOW THE MEETING ENDED:

with a yes
a sorry-not-right-now,
and my
loud-ass sighs
the whole ride home.
                                 But still I felt frigg'n amazing.
Because . . .

If that night of overdrinking with #TeamMerc,
and that morning of *Family Feud* after
broke me,
and filled me with doubt,

then that day with our moms meeting
Merc in the city
put me back together again.
For real.

Now Ma just needed
to sign the damn contract!

01905554848: How was that?

Dali: You were perfect, corazoncito.

Me: Yeah, YOU were. My mom? Not so much.

Dali: See you when you get back from LA?

01905554848: Sure thing. And Denver, get mama dukes n check, aight? Can't have Say Say goin solo. ☺

ONCE UPON A TIME,

there lived a mom
and a dad
and a sister
and an other.

The mom
and dad
and Gwen
fit into a perfect box.

Each line straight,
each angle perfectly
perpendicular.

But an other was just that.
The other.
Crooked.
Bent.
Jagged.

One day the mom
and the dad
packed the sister
and the Other.

Big city left behind,
whisked away
to mountain-covered
country,
better schools (& brand-new jobs).

Full of hope that
the Other would
learn and mold
and fit
into this new box
they squeezed her in.

Little did they know,
the Other
would go on
to build her own.

THAT CONTRACT

sat on the kitchen counter
collecting cereal crumbs
for what felt like
two thousand
seventy-leven
days.

Un   bothered
Un   impressed
Un   touched

"DID MERC TEXT YOU LAST NIGHT?"

Dali shoved a spoonful
of cookies & cream
in her mouth.

It was Netflix night at her crib.
Just me, her, and no Shak.
Still wasn't used to that.

"Text about what?"
                    "He's back from LA
                    and ready to work.
                    Studio time is booked for next week.
                    And get this . . . he's sending a car service!

                    "Mami was all:
                    Dios mío, this guy's
                    the REAL DEAL, eh?

                    "She already said I could go
                    but she's not trying
                    to miss another day of work.
                    So what's up? You coming?"

Here was the thing:
Merc didn't hit me up,
didn't invite me to jack,
and I knew exactly why.

"Nah, next time."
                    Dali flung her hair
                    across my lap,
                    lay on top of me,
                    lips all pouty.
                    "I don't like that idea, Denver."

"Yeah. Me neither."
                    I clicked play
                    on *Jane the Virgin*,
                    stuffed an Oreo
                    down my throat,
                    and tried my best to pretend
                    that shit didn't taste like
                    disappointment.

SATURDAY, JULY 27

8:30 p.m.
no sooner than you
walked through the door
I popped off with
questions about that contract
my dreams
my future

The why? (weren't you at the meeting, Papi)
The how? (could you forget about me)
The WHEN? (would you and Ma sign)

Every answer
that cascaded off
your lips
sounded like a
running list of synonyms
for the word
NOPE!

Instead, you had
something else on your mind.

"Denver?
Your mother and I
have something to tell you . . ."

SHOULDA SAW IT

coming years ago.

See, pretending is a talent
we got on lock.

The perfect picture of
a happy family:
the successful doctor
with her successful pilot husband
their *one* successful daughter

Gwendolyn Jaylis Lafleur:
Maker of dean's list,
Doer of nothing wrong,

and the Other,
singer of emo-ass songs,
player of instruments,
which was cute,
but not enough to do enough.

The greatest show on Earth
was the one where on the outside
things seemed good,
till you grabbed a microscope,
looked deep,

saw the tiny crack
stretching its way
through years of "missed flights" home
and late nights at the hospital.

When I was younger,
I didn't see these things.

But time passed,
and the cracks multiplied,
heavy under the weight
of pretending.

SEPARATION:

that funny little word
that came before

D
   I
      V
        O
          R
            C
              E

             All those years

    of   stretched out days,
endless nights,
I listened to Ma
cry for you
to come back
as you barreled out
the front door,
while I looked out my bedroom window,
wishing you'd take me with you,
watched you
drive off to
godknowswhere
beneath a midnight sky;

your absence
a disease,

your presence
a present
for all of us.

It wasn't
the first time
I'd heard
y'all say
you were done.

             It was just

the first time
I believed you.

SEPARATION

was also code for:
that contract
and my dreams
didn't mean jack

Because it didn't fit the vision
of what life would look like
for me
for Gwen
for YOU.
(and Ma)

"BUT DO YOU GUYS

care about what I said?
Dali is going to record without me!

You're sabotaging my future
because *your* marriage sucks!"

I expected to feel
the sting of a hand
against my cheek,

a hard grip on my arm,
fiery words
to extinguish my own.

                              Instead

                Ma hustled
            to her bedroom,
cigarette smoke
building beneath
closed doors,
then curling,
swirling through
every crevice like a whole mood.

And you, Papi, stormed off,
yet again

tires skidding
over unpaved roads . . .

I headed to the basement,
let it out
the best way I knew how:
lights dimmed
candles lit
fingers plucked Em chords,
ready to record.

                              The thing about
                                    music was
                              once it sparked,
                              lyrics unfolded,
                                    a prelude
                                    to a flame
                        that refused to die.

I'M THROUGH

Written by Denver Lafleur

Verse:

I always do what you say
Put aside my dreams every day
I give my time,
sacrifice my life,
Just so you could fly
Now I wonder when
I can begin
to shine my light within

Pre-chorus:

Starting today,
I'll find my way

Chorus:

I'm through with you,
through with you
through with you, ooh
I'm through with your rules
I'm putting me first
'cause I know my worth

I BELTED OUT THAT LAST NOTE,

                                                            veins breaking
                                                          through skin
                        Turned off the record button,
                        pulled up Dali's and one of Merc's
                        many numbers,
                        clicked send

                  Heard the basement door crack,
                        footsteps descend

Smelled the
smoky stench
before I saw Ma's face

"Merc's right, Denver. Your talent is endless.
I know this little singing thing
is important to you. Just like it was for your father
when he tried to be a musician at your age.
But jazz was never gonna pay the bills.
We just need more time to decide."

Little.
Of course that's
all I heard.

                        Little music
                        Little phase
                        Little dream

I forced myself
to remember a time
she ever listened to my music,
stuck around,
showed up.
Came up empty.

We stood like mirrors,
ocean meeting earth,
my eyes
a reflection of
both hers and yours, Papi.

              Hurting
                Wordless
                      Truth unfolding . . .
Not sure
I had much time left.

Gwen: Denny, you up? I'm so sorry I haven't been returning your calls. Been so busy with interning and getting ready for next semester abroad.

12:29 a.m.

Gwen: I heard the news about them separating. Wish I was there with you.

12:33 a.m.

Gwen: You should get away for a while. My dorm is open. Think about it?

12:48 a.m.

Me: Sis, Ma started smoking cigarettes again. I think it's for real for real this time.

Gwen: I know. ☹

UNDER A BLACK SKY,

void of stars and moon,
there was a girl who quietly
slipped out of her home
on Chickasaw Lane,
walked past the Trails End sign
dimly lit at the exit,

crossed Route 6,
sharp left on Springwood Drive,
followed each curve,
in long, hurried steps,
until she reached Winding Brook Road,
the crunch of gravel beneath her feet.

Quietly, she climbed the ladder
on the side of the big house
with the double red doors,
until she reached the flattened roof

fingers tap-tap-tapped the bedroom window,
~~awakening~~ rescuing me
from the nightmare, skin-deep.

"Dali, what are you doing here?"

"I heard your song.
No way I'm leaving you alone.
Olive juice."

THAT NIGHT

as we lay in my bed,
curtains drawn back,
fingers exploring
parts where pain
once dwelled,
two dueling meteor showers
lit up Pennsylvania skies.

A silent, wordless
burst of magic
that was our universe,
that was . . . us.

There was no need to
tell Dali what went down
with you and Ma earlier.

The lyrics,
the music
communicated it all
through
      bitten lips,
           bursting stars,
                beating hearts . . .
a thousand different ways.

SOME

times
unabashed
love
only
reveals
itself
under
darkened
skies,
satin   sheets,   words   unspoken,   behind   locked   doors

. . .

An aria in the key of denial
Written by us both

The next day,
that black Mercedes SUV
cruised through Trails End
music bumping,
thumping off hip-hop beats.

I had a good mind
to ignore you and Ma,
hop in that ride with her
and head to the studio.

"Don't worry," Dali said.
"They'll come around."

The driver stepped out,
suited up, blazer, bow tie, hat and all
just like in the movies.

Folks in the trailer park
stopped and stared
as the driver reached Dali's doorstep.

"Right this way, Ms. Gómez."
He opened the door.
"Per Mr. Ellis's request,
I'll hold on to your cell phone.
He prefers that you study your lyrics."

Dali handed over that phone,
a look painted on her face like
How will I even survive????

And honestly, I wondered the same.

A DOZEN THOUGHTS

raced through me
a disastrous remix of

imnotokay
thisisnotokay
ishouldbegoing
~~notyou~~
withyou

                              Especially since
                              meeting Merc would've
                              never happened without . . . *me.*

But the mere thought
seemed selfish, wrong.

So the proper thing
to do was

wave
smile
stand at the
edge of the driveway

watching
Dali
and
~~my~~ her chauffeur
and my lyrics
literally drive away

                              Suspense
                    ate away at my nerves,
              hours passed,
no word from Dali.

I missed everything that night.
The pulse of the music,
soaking in chords, notes, melodies.
Meanwhile, Ma didn't even come home.
Nor did you, Papi.
Typical.

Dali:

Home now.

He loved your new song,

but barely let me sing any leads.

Denver, I need you with me next time.

K?

Me:

k.

One thing
I'd never done
was broken a promise to Dali

Ever.
No sense in starting.

ONCE UPON A TIME

there lived a girl
who stared NO in the face,
laughed at that shit,
and took matters
into her own hands.

A song in the key of *DO YOU, BOO!*
By Denver Lee Lafleur

OPERATION GET IT DONE

And by *it*,
I mean that contract.

Step 1: Read it (See, Papi, I *did* study sometimes!)

Absorb all of it—
those
mixed-up,
mashed-up
words
like
foreign-language
too hard,
too trapped
beneath thick tongues

Step 2: Sign it

Because the longer
I left my future
in your hands,
the quicker it was gonna
slip

a
      w
          a
             y

Step 3: Send it

One click of a button
loud enough to
let Merc know
that this life,
this dream,
wasn't worth
stalling a second more.

01905552702: Aye, superstar! I see u got ur folks n check.

Me: Sure did.

01905552702: oh, baby gurl 😒😒☺

Me: ?

01905552702: Denver, I know your handwriting.

12:51 p.m.

01905552702: u there?

Me: BUT THEY LEFT ME NO CHOICE. Guess you're done with me now???

01905552702: Nah, we just getn started. ☺

THESE WERE THE THINGS

I couldn't unsee:

the passing of time,
no ginger-spiced
Saturday mornings,
no bittersweet
Sunday goodbyes
with you . . .

Ma slipping
into that sunken place,
a bottomless pit
of *woe-is-freakin-me.*

A zombie
of a woman
playing
work-sleep-wait
on

Repeat
Repeat
                            A convenience for me tho,

                    the perfect excuse
            to dip off
sight unseen
            to the studio.

New songs in my journal,
Dali at my side,
Merc with the sick beats.

Time did not exist
when I was there with them

Eventually
I figured
Ma (or you) would notice
I was gone
—a bit too much—
But right then and there
I had'ta do what was best for ME.

Memories
were like water.

Life giving,
soul filling,
moment in time.

Easy to be forgotten,
if you couldn't hold them tight.

Maybe that's why
I started to notice
that camcorder,
almost always at Merc's side.

With it, a duffel bag
filled with VHS-C tapes,
mini golden treasures,
epic adventures,
in the studio,
on the road,
fans screaming,
songs written.

Merc said that Panasonic
PVL453 was the first
thing he purchased
when he hit it big.
And it was way
too precious to part with.
Plus it still worked.

I guess every celebrity
has their weird must-haves.

To me,
camcorders were on the
ancient end of the technology spectrum.
Maybe they'd be worth a grip in the future.

Then again,
maybe not.

Merc brought in a heavy hitter
to help produce the final cut
of our newest song,

"I'm Through."

Bryan Lewis,
hitmaker to the stars,
white boy in a Bob Marley disguise,
comin' straight outta Australia
just to work with Untouched.

fifty-leven takes
was all it took
to hear those magic words
through my headphones.

"I think we're all done, Denver!
Merc will love it."

Meat opened the door of the booth.
"Sounding real good, girl!" He beamed.
"You can come on out now."

I zombie-walked
my way past the control board,
Bryan dapping me up,
before I collapsed on the couch
wishing Dali were there to catch my fall.

Instead, she was
in studio B, down the hall,
recording backgrounds on our next
song for the last two hours.

"Where's me ole mate, Merc?
He needs to hear this!"
Bryan played the track from the top.

Mannn, that bass kicked in
followed by the tap-tap-tap
of the drum
and then that voice.
All buttery and,
dare I say, *Whitneyish*.
But all mine.

Next thing I knew,
I was up on my feet
swerving to the beat,
hardly believing that that was me.

Bryan busted a move, too,
dreads swinging,
beatboxing!

Even Meat
couldn't resist a two-step,
awkward as his giant self looked.

                              "Oh, your voice is sick, Denver!"
                              Bryan yelled over the bass.
                              "I'm going to the Bottle-O downstairs
                              for a pack of ciggies.
                              Can I get you anything?"

"I'm good," I said.
"I'm just ready for Dali
and Merc to hear this joint!"

Bryan nodded
and shortly after he bounced,
the song began to fade out,
and I wanted to hear it
again and again
until every note sank to my bones.

                    I took a seat in Bryan's chair,
                    the wide computer screen
                    drinking me in,
                    ran my fingers over the mouse.

"Tsk tsk, Denver.
You know not to touch the equipment."

                    I swiveled in Meat's direction,
put on my best Dali
                    bat-my-lashes, smile-like-the-devil voice:
                    "I just want a copy of my song.
                    Not a sample. Come on! You know it's a hit!"

Arms pretzeled tight.
"You tryna get me fired?
Merc and the girls went to grab food.
They'll probably be back any minute."
                    I did that blink-and-pout thing on repeat.

"Don't you look at me with those eyes!"

Hit him with that combo once more.

Then he started laughing.
"I got a cousin with heterochromia, too,

'cept she got one gray, one green eye.
But the answer is still no."

                    "Would you kill your cousin's hopes like that?"

Meat dragged his hand
across his bearded face,
shifted on his feet,
cracked the door open
and looked down the empty hall.
                    "You got like two and a half minutes, girl."

I jumped out the chair
hands in the air,
ready to hug that teddy bear,
dressed in muscle disguise,
          but he hit me with the Wakanda arms
          hella quick.
          "You betta not tell Merc about this."

REASON #145 WHY I'M SMART

(contrary to popular belief)

A true artist never
leaves the house
without her tools.

Which is why
in my pink AliExpress bag,
behind the song journals
and
      pens
and
      pads
and
      packs of gum,

there lie a tiny
SanDisk flash drive,
hidden in the
small zipper compartment.

64 GB,
to be exact,
large enough to hold
the MP3 file of
the song
that was gonna
change our lives—
my life
forever.

One click,
5 megs,
a hurried download
of epic proportions,
Supermanned my ass
back to the couch,
SanDisk tucked away,
just in time
for that door to swing open . . .

         "We've got ourselves a piss-up now!"
           Bryan walked in, cigarette dangling
           from his thin lips,
           a six-pack of Dos Equis in each hand,

Merc and Marissa
trailing behind him,

hands full of McDonald's bags.

       That cheesy, salty,
       oniony smell filling the space,
       throwing my senses all off balance.

I locked eyes with Meat
for a split second,
the look we shared,
a reciprocal whisper
of *shutyodamnmouth*.

          "I thought Dali was with you?" I asked.

Merc plopped next to me on the couch.
"Nah, she's done for the night.
Asked to take a nap
before y'all bounce.
Ay yo, Bryan, run the track."

          Bryan clicked play,
          volume on simmer mode this time,
          while we bopped our heads,
          cracked open the beers
          and those McDonald's bags.

Merc handed me mine,
I ripped that thing open
ready to dive in to a Big Mac
only to realize he ordered me
a Supersize McNope . . .
          As in a damn garden salad.

I could feel the
color of my skin shift
light brown to crimson.

          "Just tryna get you
          ready for prime time, baby gurl."

Merc quick-tapped my belly,
making it jiggle right along
with my bottom lip.

I tugged at my T-shirt,
pushing it deeper into my belt.

          Marissa giggled a toothy laugh,
          but no one else did.

And suddenly I was no longer hangry.

        In fact, everybody
        was hella silent as the track
        played and played until it
        faded into nothingness.

"Well, thanks for the burgers,
but it's time for me to
head back to my hotel.
Early flight tomorrow.
Catch you later, mate?"
Bryan started gathering
his things.

        "Meat can drive you back." Merc stood,
        dapping Bryan up. "Marissa, you can head out, too."

I felt myself
fold further
into myself on the couch
as I painted on a weak smile,
said my thank-yous and goodbyes,
until all that was left behind
was just me and Merc
and that insult.

        "You didn't have to play me like that,"
        I whispered, eyes glued to the floor,
        trying my hardest not to cry.

"Oh, baby gurl,
don't get so caught up.
You're beautiful just the way you are."

        I sat straighter,
        only a little though.

"But you see, this music thing
ain't just about the music.

"It's equal parts discipline,
eating right,
waist snatched,
wardrobe on point,
leveling up your game,
musically,
lyrically,
physically . . .

"Least, that's what all the *big* stars
do. Every day, Denver."

I thought about
every magazine cover,
red carpet,
every music video
I'd ever seen.

Beyoncé,
Cardi,
Queen Yeli,
all of them,
flesh and curves,
beat to the gods.
   A silhouette of perfection
   that would never be meant for me.
   And I was always fine with that . . .
   until recently.

"Now come on, eat, baby gurl.
You need your strength."

Slowly, I lifted the
fork to my lips,
swallowed that bland-ass salad down
and pretended like it was
the juiciest burger I ever had.

Merc stuffed a wad of fries in his mouth,
replayed our songs on low
all over again.

The air shifted
warmth replaced chill,
like a whole mood
filling the space.

And then . . .
Merc transformed into
an open book
on full display, just for me.

A subtle reminder of
our connection from that first day
at the studio,

   And I don't mean in the way
   Ma thought—

That whole grown-ass-man-
hanging-with-teenage-girls thing.

It wasn't like that with Merc.

I'm talking 'bout
the night when gravity
disappeared beneath my feet
and he guided me through
every missed note,
          every off-key melody.

It was then
that I knew
what we had
was on another level.

                    "Back in the day,
               I was the shy kid
             living in the projects,
        apartment crawling with roaches."
     Merc popped another fry in his mouth.

          "I never was a good student,"
                    he admitted,
and I nodded,
'cause I felt that deep in my soul.

"I hate math the most." I laughed.

          "Nah. Reading was the worst."

And I felt that one, too.
'Specially with summer school.
               "See, me and you?"
          Merc touched his temple.
               "Only reading we
                    care about
               is notes on bars."

If you looked up the word
twin
in the dictionary,
I was convinced
there'd be a pic of Merc and me.

               "I wasn't like them
               other kids, Denver."

Instead of going out to play,
Merc stayed in the house
creating songs,
melodies,
a way OUT.

For some folks

OUT meant . . .
you made it big-time
too good-for-the-hood:
Money,
Fame,
Cars,
Clothes,
Paparazzi,
sniffing up your ass.

"That's why you gotta
just do what I say & trust my intentions.
People will talk about you,
make up lies,
anything to cop a dollar
off what you built
with your bare hands.

"And that's why
I'm so protective of
y'all."

His voice, mad sincere.
Every part of me
digested that convo.
(right along with them slimy-ass tomatoes)

And I got it.
All of it.
I wished you and Ma could get it, too.

Dali finally came in the studio,
eyes barely open,
yawning on repeat.

"We should get going," I said,
grabbing my pink backpack,
pupils widening at the memory
of what I'd done behind Merc's back.
The voice inside whispering,

That song was yours to take.

"You guys are welcome to stay," he said.
"Got plenty of rooms."

But with two hours to get back to Shohola,
slip in the house before Tía Esme,
staying was not an option.

Always the gentleman,
Merc rode the elevator with us downstairs.

In the tightness of the space,
I could feel him staring down at me,
and then he touched my backpack.

Heartbeat in full 8-count mode
I tried my best to smile and pretend
like that flash drive didn't exist.

"I'ma have to get you a new purse, baby gurl.
Where'd you get this? Walmart?"

"Close enough!" Dali giggled.

And I didn't know if
I shoulda laughed or swallowed
that ball building in my throat.
"It's my favorite," I said.
"It's precious, kinda like that camera of yours."

That made Merc smile
wide enough to cover his whole face.

The elevator doors opened,
Dali and I rushing out.
"Hey, Denver!" Merc growled.

My feet screeched,
whole body jolted.

                "Forgetting something?"
I turned around
to Merc's dimply smirk,
and me and Dali's cell phones
dangling from his hands.
                "Oh. Yeah. Thanks."
                We grabbed those phones
                and booked it outta there.

Fast as feet could fly,
we zoomed to the Hudson parking lot.

"Why you acting all jumpy?"
Dali huffed beside me.

                "*Gurrrrl*, you'll never believe what I did!"

"Oh, DO tell, amiga . . ."

                Soon as I did,
                there wasn't enough horsepower
                to get us through the Lincoln Tunnel,
                down 287,
                up Route 6,
                all the way to Trails End,
                where Dali's laptop waited
                for my flash drive,
                fully loaded with a
                little,
                stolen,
                musical treasure.

                A crime of petty proportions
                that we both agreed I'd never
                commit again.

IN AUGUST,

the Shohola air
reeked of the worst
odor in the world:
SCHOOL.

Any other year,
y'all woulda spent
the summer
up my ass
telling me to study,
read,
hired private tutors
to get my whole life together.

But that summer
was when both of y'all
took the lazy route,
checked in for like five seconds,
then checked all the way
O
U
T

Focus shifted to
trying to seal up the cracks,
Krazy Glue your faces
into a permanent
"Everything is all right" smile.
When it wasn't.

'Cause for y'all
the world—aka the folks back home—
was watching,
waiting
for the too-good-for-the-hood
Lafleurs
to go tumbling
d
  o
       w
      n .

Soon as we wrapped up a session,
Merc hit us with this piece of gold:
"Y'all should come on the road with me."

"You mean like to your concerts and stuff?"
Dali couldn't hold in the excitement.

"Concerts, video shoots, all of it.
And you could stay in Atlanta
—that's the hot spot for artists.
I'd set y'all up real nice,
with your own space in the crib."

Sneaking out
all summer
turned out to
be easy enough.
(epic showdown with the Browns aside)

In bed before the sun rose,
before anyone noticed or cared
that we had been out all night.

But this?
This was different.

As in,
let's-run-away-from-home
and-pray-y'all-won't-kill-us
different.

Then again,
you knew a lil' sumthin-sumthin
'bout running away, too,
didn't you, Papi?

FOUR THINGS I LOVED ABOUT WORKING WITH MERC

1. The music—three songs down, two more to go, to finish our demo before he'd shop it to record labels
2. The education—better than anything I'd ever get at school
3. The gifts—dude kept us stacked with the freshest kicks, jewelry, and clothes
4. The dream—that I got to live out with Dali at my side

Four things I hated:

1.
2.
3.
4.

(nothing)

NEW SONG TITLE: SECURITY

Written by ~~Denver Lafleur~~ Sean "Mercury" Ellis

Verse:

Been wanting this for a long time
Gonna take my chance
I'm done with pretending,
it's time to start mending
the heart
you tore apart

All good, 'cause I'm secure now
I gotta go . . .

Chorus:

It's time to leave
I know it's hard to believe
Don't be scared for me
'Cause I got security

A place to go that's all mine
cash money on flow
Ya little girl will be fine

Day & night
'cause I got security (security)

wrapped up recording my new song.
Once again, Merc didn't change the lyrics.
Just slapped his name on the credits,
'cause according to our contract,
that was "standard practice."

"In this industry,
new peeps get no love,
until they get a stamp of approval
from someone big like me."

Soon enough though
Merc promised my name would be on
ev-er-ee-thang we put out!

And I wouldn't have to sneak
to download my work,
and live with the guilt of doing so.

All I had to do was prove myself
as an artist,
worthy and true.

I knew my time was coming.
For real, for real.

In a perfect world

I would have controlled time.
It moved too fast,
raced parallel to my thoughts,
crashing into decisions,
scenarios,
the endless
what-if?

Like . . .

What if me and Dali could convince y'all to let us go?
(Instead of us just dipping off?)
What woulda happened if y'all said no?
Would Merc forget about us, and find the next best thing?

'Cause like he said,
every
body
is replaceable.

Those questions

percolated in our minds
as we did the math of how long we had to act.

Thirteen days before ~~torture~~ school started
Soon enough, Merc would hit the road—

whether we rolled or not.
The verdict was in:
Dali and I couldn't let that happen.

we needed a plan,
a proper way to say
goodbye.

Of course, I figured it out,
told Merc about it
right before we wrapped up
in the studio.

"Oh, baby gurl, that's perfect."
Merc whipped out his phone,
started pressing buttons like mad.

"What're you doing?"
Dali tried to peek over his shoulder,
but he pulled away,
big grin slapped on his face.

"Chill, Say Say.
Just a little something
to put that plan in effect.
You'll see when you get your phones
on the way out." He winked, walked down the hall,
and disappeared behind one
of the doors.

Meat escorted us to the first floor,
where Marissa waited,
our Androids in each hand.
"Safe travels home,"
she muttered and then clicked the buzzer.
We headed outside,
frozen in August heat,
among hustling,
bustling New York streets,
and waited for our phones to turn on,
notifications ringing in perfect unison:
A $1,500 deposit from Cash App!

An email in our inboxes:
Two tickets to Atlanta
FIRST class!
"OMGOMGOMG!"
we screamed
loud enough to pierce
a hole through the sky.

Jumped up and down,
tilted our heads to the sun.
Ten floors above
Merc stood,
half his body
dangling out the window.

"How's that for a plan?"
his voice thunder-
bolted city streets.

"Thank you, papi-i-i-i!"
Dali sang that last bit
full-chest voice,
jazz scat
rich enough to
make Ella Fitzgerald
rise from the dead.

If my
feet could
grow wings,
I woulda
flew up there,
squeezed
the hell outta
Merc
till he couldn't
breathe.

Of course
he went all out for us,
the next stars in his universe.
Merc wouldn't have it
any other way.

SATURDAY, AUGUST 10

                              Goodbyes
               were permanent.
But *see you soon?*

Well, that
sounded better,
hopeful,
something to cling on to.

IN THE LITTLE BROWN TRAILER

on Chickasaw Lane,
$1,500
perfectly placed
on Tía Esme's altar,
like a palm tree,
a fan, of sorts,
to cool the words
written
in the language
of love,
ink bleeding slowly
on the paper beneath it.

> Querida Mami,
> Un regalo, para ti.
> Con amor,
> Dalisay

I took the tips of my fingers,
ran them through Dali's hair,
making music out of it,
like a harp,
woven down
chin,
shoulder,
arm,
hand.

"We could stay, if you want."

"No.
Mami will be happy for the gift.
There's more coming,
Merc will make sure of it."

Backpack gripped
on stiff shoulders,
Dali slid the trailer door shut,
and didn't look back.

MEANWHILE,

on a granite countertop
on Winding Brook Road . . .
there sat

A VASE
filled with calla lilies.
(Ma's favorite)

A REPORT
of my online summer school GPA
—3.06—not bad, right?
and

A LETTER
written to you both

> Dear Ma and Papi,
> I'll make you proud. You'll see.
> Denver

I left that $1,500 right in my possession,
because let's be honest,
did y'all even need it?

Tossed our luggage in the trunk
of my Honda Civic,
stuck the key in the ignition,
and before I pulled off,
whipped out my phone.

Me: Sis, hope the offer still stands. Me and Dali are on our way.

Gwen: OMG are you serious? Yay!

Me: But I got a secret and I'ma need you to keep it.

Gwen: You mean from Detective Ma? LOL! What is it?

Me: Tell you when I get there. You owe me this one.

Gwen: I know. DON'T REMIND ME. Geez!

Me: See you in a few hours. ♡

HIDDEN DEEP

beneath the 4.0 GPA,
the scholarships,
clubs,
sports,
teams,

there once lived
a sister with a secret
of her own.
                    A classic high school tale
            of boy meets girl.

Chandler Pierce:
Captain of the football team
with the river-green eyes
that turned chicks
into human puddles of
omg-he's-so-frigg'n-hawt!

Gwen Lafleur:
Valedictorian by day,
Chandler's brown little boo thang by night

A love (lust?)
tended to
beneath dark skies
where no one else could see

And by no one,
I mean Chandler's
Confederate-flag-waving parents.

And you, Papi, with your
"no dating until twenty-five"
and "don't even THINK
about bringing no white boy home"
policies.

REAL LOVE LOOKED LIKE . . .

Hands on belly, brimming with heat
both hearts taking turns to beat
A longing look that begged

What if we're making the wrong decision?
What if we keep it? (her?) (him?)

Real love looked like
soft tissues mopping up
falling tears

waiting for the nurse
to call out:

Patient Gwendolyn Lafleur?
Right this way.

Chandler wasn't there for none of that . . .
but I was.

304.8 MILES LATER,

Dartmouth College was . . .

Too   green
Too   rich
Too   smart
Too   quiet
Too

       CORNY

             for

                  my

                       Black

                             ass!

DARTMOUTH WAS ALSO

a reminder
of all that you and Ma
had ever dreamed for us.

You both went there,
so you expected us to do
the same.

Gwen followed in your footsteps.
As for me?
Well, I never been one for tradition.
(but you knew that, didn't you?)

                              When receiving a hug
            from a sister you
                    hadn't seen in months,
it was best to
lower expectations
of breathing.

                  "I can't WAIT to show you guys around!"
                  Gwen peeped.

Our campus tour
was a stretch of:

Collis Center
The Hop
Leede Arena
Baker-Berry Library

and the Organic Farm
where they made homemade pizza.

In other words,
the tour was a big yawnfest.
Pizza was bangin' tho.

"Bet you two
want to apply here now!"

I almost spat my food out laughing.

                  "Nah, we wanna see the world," Dali reminded Gwen.

"But you can,
which is why I'm
studying abroad
in Paris starting next month.
Putting our French to work, Denny!"

See what I mean?
Perfect. Freak'n. Daughter . . .

                    Three amigas
            sprawled out on the grass
      in front of Dartmouth Hall,
pepperoni wasted.

Sun hidden within clouds,
a breezy battle of
heat and cool.

"So tell me, guys.
What's the big secret?
I can't wait a second longer . . ."

MY FOUR FAVORITE REACTIONS

1. Damn girl! You waited this long to tell me THAT?
2. PLEASE take me with you!
3. Wait. They don't know? You want me to tell them WHAT?
4. Girl, Ma and Papi are gonna KILL you something good.

Gwen: Attention parental units: Denny and Dali came up for a college tour! They'll stay on campus with me for a week-ish.

Papi: Bon nouvel! Good news! Best way to celebrate your birthday, Denver!

Ma: THANK YOU FOR THE NOTE, REPORT CARD, & FLOWERS. PROUD OF YOU, DENVER!!! EDUCATION FIRST. MUSIC CAN WAIT. PRIORITIES!

Me: Don't worry. I'm finally getting my priorities straight. Wishing the same for us all.

Ma: ???

Me: Love y'all.

SUNDAY, AUGUST 11

A promise is a promise

The next morning,
I placed my car keys in Gwen's hand,
she held on to mine two seconds
too long,
staring me down
with those begging brown eyes.
"You sure about this?"
I'd never been so sure in my life.

"You just better be the first one
to pump the hell out of our
music when it drops!"

"Consider it done."

Our private car pulled up—
a white Cadillac Escalade stretch limo—

The driver grabbed our bags.
Gwen folded me and Dali in her arms.

"Be safe.
And, Denny? Happy (early) birthday."

We hopped in the limo
and made our way to
Manchester airport.

Phone on mute
because nothing else
mattered at that point.

Eyes to the sky.
I knew I'd be up there soon.

IT WAS VIP FROM JUMP

the second we arrived:
Miss Lafleur,
Miss Gómez,
follow us!

The airport greeters took our bags,
zipped us through check-in,
security, and straight to the lounge.

Leather recliner seats
Floor-to-ceiling windows
A full view of the runway
First-class seats on the plane

> "A bon voyage drink,
> compliments of Mr. Ellis,"
> the waiter said.

Merc had magic like that.
He wasn't even there
and he was taking care of us!

I took a slow sip,
let the alcohol-free
coolness work its way down.

Wished it was something harder
to wash away the small piece
of doubt that still remained.

Taking a deep breath,
I closed my eyes.
Dreamt of the future,
thinking of the past.

> Like that summer of eighth grade.

> A sky full of stars,
> twinkling in summer heat

Lips touched
One second,
two?

An electric jolt
stopped
before it went too far.

A whispered promise
we'd never mention it again.

                              But some words
                    had a way
               of building up
inside
               even if they never
                         crawled their way
OUT.

SPEAKING OF WORDS,

it was only right
to try one last time
to fill the empty spaces
with hope.
Dali's request.

One final group text,
one last attempt
to let Shak know
that no matter what happened
in the past
that wouldn't change the fact
that together we built
memories
to last us our whole lives.

Me: Shak, it's been too long. We love you. And miss you.

Dali: And we forgive you, too.

Me: Hope you can forgive us one day?

Dali: We're leaving for a little while.

Shak: Before y'all do something stupid, tell me one thing. How well do y'all know Merc?

Dali: Umm . . . very.

Shak: https://thedailygossip.com/parent-claims-merc-holding-daughter-captive

Written By: The Daily Gossip Staff

PARENTS CLAIM SEAN "MERCURY" ELLIS IS HOLDING DAUGHTER CAPTIVE

During his 24-year career, Sean "Mercury" Ellis has sold nearly 50 million albums.

But it wasn't always this way. Born in the inner city of Crenshaw, California, Ellis was raised in a single-parent home with seven siblings. Poverty and gangs plagued Ellis's childhood. His mother raised him and his siblings in the church, where he honed his vocal and instrumental skills. At the age of fifteen, his soul-stirring performance on Showtime at the Apollo resulted in a production deal with Vibe Records. The rest, as they say, is history. Five Grammy awards, two Billboards, and a whopping seven American Music Awards.

But the cost of fame is high. In 2006, a videotape was discovered that allegedly featured Ellis and an unnamed minor engaging in sexual activity. The case, which took three years to go to trial, resulted in Ellis being acquitted of the charges because there was no evidence or testimony to verify that it was indeed him on the tape. This, however, did not derail his career. Instead, the case and dropped charges made him more successful in the R&B/hip-hop community.

Since then, Ellis has been hailed as a savior of sorts, having been responsible for the rise of such popular artists as Lil' Mega and Shades of Black. Collaborations with megastars in pop and country have increased Ellis's popularity and crossover appeal.

Now rumors are starting to swirl again. In an exclusive interview, the parents of a young woman we'll call M allege that Ellis is holding their daughter captive.

"I haven't seen or heard from my daughter in six years." M's mother claims Ellis met her daughter at a Chicago video shoot. The 19-year-old left home shortly after.

In response to the accusation, Ellis's publicist, Raymond Markowitz III, stated, "This woman and her husband have contacted our office on two occasions threatening to sue if Mr. Ellis did not provide hush money for 'kidnapping' their daughter. It is unfortunate when ill-intentioned people insist on defaming an artist who adores his fans and works tirelessly to give back to his community. Perhaps that is the price of fame, but please respect Mr. Ellis's basic right to privacy, by ignoring unfounded rumors."

I COMBED THROUGH EVERY WORD,

hearing that
know-it-all sass in
Shak's voice,
thinking back to
all the other times
she was wrong about Merc.
I wished I could press
the mute button in my brain.

Sure he was a little strict,
but perseverance breeds results.
Didn't take a genius to understand that!
And you know what?

We tried with Shak.
Tried to do the right thing.
Be nice.
Make amends.

But the truth was clear as day.
Shakira Brown was a hater.
        Guess she always had been.
        Took her
        sending me that
        lying-ass article
        to finally see it.

I couldn't wait to show Merc
that garbage *in person*!
He warned me
about how
some folks flip the script
when you're on the come-up:

The second they see it,
they do anything to knock you down!

I scrolled through my contact list,
till I got to the letter *S*.

Mannnnn, my fingers couldn't hit
that delete button fast enough!

PART THREE: TAKEOFF

Monday, December 23
Atlanta International Airport
Time: 9:26 a.m.
Destination: Home

ALL THOSE MONTHS AGO,

I took off,
only to *take off* again,
but this time with you.

We're boarding now, Papi,
and though we won't be
seated together
—you gotta step up your pilot perks, bruh—

I'll spend this flight
praying that you'll hear
the apologies running
through my head,
feel the cold darkness fade
and the light pour in,
as I beg for a do-over.

I-85 North:

I had never
ever
ever
ever
seen a highway
THAT congested.

Dear Atlanta,
I'm gonna need y'all to get it together!

Signed,
Ya girl Denver

GPS

might have been
the biggest lie
ever invented!

A forty-two-minute ride
from the airport
was really code for:
Might as well take a two-hour NAP!

ALPHARETTA, GEORGIA

(A Suburb of Atlanta)

home to
Tyler Perry,
Ne-Yo,
Usher,
Whitney Houston,
Merc,
and now ...
US!

In other words,
welcome to
Black Hollywood!

IRON GATE,

tips dipped
in 24-carat gold,
closed tight.

Stayed that way
till the voice
waiting on the
other side of that intercom
heard the driver say:

*Denver Lee Lafleur
and Dalisay Gómez
have arrived for Mr. Ellis.*

The buzzer rang,
gates opened,

chrome wheels
rolled against
smooth pavement,
snaked its way
past sky-kissing trees,
a pond filled with koi fish,
basketball court to the left,
tennis to the right,

me and Dali,
arms linked,
100 percent
GEEKING OUT
till we reached the front steps
of the biggest house I had ever
seen in all my life.

waited at the door for us,
my disappointment settling
that it wasn't Merc.

She led us to a two-story foyer,
chandelier elevated,
each crystal
capturing a piece of the Earth's sun.

Soon as she opened
those puckered hot-pink lips of hers,
the midnight of her words
swallowed daylight whole.

"I'ma need your phones, ladies."
One hand out,
the other propped on her hip.

"What for?" Dali asked.
"Ain't like we recording right now."

"Yeah," I said,
"we're actually gonna
be staying up in this piece.
Can't live without our phones.
How are we supposed to call our—"

But then the sun in our universe walked in,

muting all
my words.

Merc had that camcorder in his hand
finger pressing the record button in
3 . . . 2 . . .
"Welcome home, my stars!"
His voice echoed through the first floor.

Me and Dali squealed like schoolgirls,
ran to him
like a father gone
too long.

"How you like the crib?"
        "Oh, it's perfect!"
                "Ditto what Dali said."

"Wave to the camera, Say Say, baby gurl.
Do a little turn,
show 'em what you working with.
You too, Denver!

"Welcome to the journey of
my next multiplatinum artists,
Untouched!"

We waved and blew kisses
to imaginary fans.

Merc stopped recording
and handed the camcorder to Meat,
who secured it in that duffel bag.

"Now first order of business
I can't have y'all
rocking these old-ass phones—"

                    Marissa cut Merc off.
                    "I told them to give 'em up—"

Merc raised one hand,
and like a soldier, homegirl stood at attention.

"Now, now,
I'ma have to ease them into this.
This is new territory for them.

See I'm 'bout to take y'all on a whole journey,
and for starters, I'll need your complete attention.

"All work.
No distractions."

Merc pulled out two boxes wrapped in
a pretty pink-and-silver bow.

We opened them
like two kids on Christmas day.

Two brand-new iPhones
for us to keep with us at all times,

which woulda been cool,
'cept they had
only one saved number (Merc's),
no internet,

NO social media,

and a code
only he knew to unlock
it all when necessary.

                    "Come on, Merc! Why so extra?"
                    I couldn't help it.
                    No matter how Dali looked at me
                    with those *pleasebabyplease* eyes.

The crease around
Merc's mouth deepened.
"Never forget, baby gurl,
distractions breed failure."

"Yeah, yeah, whatever."
Shoulders went in full slump mode.

I mean, I got it.
Didn't mean I wanted to.

                    When it came to Merc's plan
                    to get us to the top,
                    Dali and I agreed there'd be

no clapback,
no compromise,
just a nod
and a yes
to give in
to his
every demand—
no matter how bad
~~we~~ I felt like popping off
at the mouth.

Because with an opportunity
of a lifetime
staring me in the face,
what other choice did I have?

Give up (and break my promise to Dali) . . .
or *lean* in? (and make my wildest dream a reality)

Uhhh-hmmm.
EXACTLY!

I may not have liked
that whole no-technology
caveman living,
but the next part
made up for it . . .

Sort of.

BEHOLD!

A walking tour through Merc's castle,
just me and Merc,
while Marissa took Dali godknowswhere:

Indoor swimming pool
Gym
Sauna

A never-ending
freaking Wonderland . . .

Barbershop
Salon
And then,
upstairs,
a ~~little~~ big palace . . .

WALLS

painted black
rhinestones scattered
to offset the darkness.

Windows dressed
in thick velvet curtains,
a bed fit for a queen
tucked in the
deepest corner of the room

A Gibson Montana Hummingbird
on top of the bed.

Next to the guitar, two journals
each one labeled: FOR YOU.
Inside inscribed:

A place to hold
lyrics waiting
to turn to gold.

Your biggest fan,
Merc

"Wow, thank you, Merc.
I can't believe you got this for us."

"Us? No. Just you.
This room and everything in it
is only for you."

> I looked around the large space,
> feeling hella small.
> "But what about Dali—"

Merc grabbed me by both hands.
"Baby gurl, you are a genius in the making.
I need you focused, separate. Say Say's talented and all,
but you? You're the real star. She'll catch up . . .
eventually."

> I felt a burn incinerate my whole chest.
> *Was that a compliment?*
> But most of all . . . *did I like it?* (yes. wait, no. right?)

Merc snapped his fingers.
"Enough about that! Take a look
around your master suite!"

In the hall, leading to
my bathroom,
a walk-in closet,
full of designer clothes,
(why did I even pack?)
shoes, jewelry,
everything I was gonna need.

A spa-like bathroom,
white marble soaking tub
to the right,
walk-in shower
with twelve jets
to the left.

And in the center of the floor,
a digital scale
staring back at me.

                    "Baby gurl
It's not that you're fat . . .
It's not that you're skinny . . .
It's just that you're . . ."

                    A lot?

Those last words didn't come out of Merc's mouth,
but I saw them in his eyes.

Once upon a time,
he called me *strong*.

"Don't worry,
I got you a trainer
and errthang.
We gonna get you *tight*!"

Merc tapped
my shoulder,
turned his back,
and headed out of my suite.

            Two feet,
        quick step on the scale.
                The numbers
                flashed bold and blue

on the screen.

I folded myself
arms to gut,
caught up to Merc in the hall,

pressed down those feelings,
(of too muchness?)
whispered to myself . . .
Just a little off the top, right?
How hard can it be?

                    Speaking of feelings

Moving in with Merc
felt like
some kind of
reality show
where the most disciplined,
most focused
ended up the winner.

Grand prize!
Set for life!
            Which wasn't far off
            from how things were
            for the Lafleurs back home . . .
            that whole #workhard #teamnosleep
            philosophy instilled since birth.

So if hard work was what
it was gonna take
to make it to the top,
then that's exactly what
I'd serve up.

                Black girl:
                        mixed with grit,
                        stardust,
                        spice,
                        magic.

DALI'S ROOM

was on the opposite end of that
big ole castle of a house.

I would
tell you what it looked like
if only I was allowed in it.

we sat on plush sofa chairs,
in front of a huge bow window
overlooking peach trees.

An older lady,
dressed in a full-on maid uniform,
brought us glasses
of something bubbly.

"Thank you, Ms. . . . what's your name?"
I asked, but she didn't even
make eye contact, nor did she respond.
Just propped up the serving tray
and hurried back to the kitchen.

Well, alrighty, then.
Dali nudged me in my side.
"Show him, muchacha."

I asked Merc
if I could use the internet,
like a goddamned kindergartner.

Marissa passed me a tablet,
I pulled up the link,
and handed it to Merc.

He squinted his eyes,
stretched the tablet back . . .
"Tell me what it says, Denver."

The whole room
Merc
Meat
Marissa
Dali

went silent,
lips sealed,
eyes open,
ears tuned in

as I read
the fiery words
of that article Shak sent.

"Captive?" Merc said.

I couldn't tell if
that was a question
or flame.

Merc couldn't hold
it any longer.
Laughter poured out
like a rushing river,
lampshades trembled
with each stomp of his foot.
Meat and Marissa
joined in like a chorus.

"Baby gurl . . . Say Say . . ."
Merc hunched over,
drowning in his own laughter,
extended a finger.

"I'd like for you to meet M."

Marissa waved at us,
a smile
big enough
to clear furniture
out the room.

THREE THINGS YOU SHOULD KNOW

(according to Marissa)

1. Does it look like I'm being held captive? Or a whole-ass woman with a job?
2. Never read (or believe) the media. It's all FAKE NEWS.
3. My parents are batshit crazy, which is why I left in the first place.

And honestly,
I was so relieved
I coulda laughed and cried
at the same damn time.

But not Dali.
She had this look
painted on her face.

"So . . . you used to sing? Not anymore?"
Dali's eyes shifted from Marissa to Merc,
lightning speed.

"Turns out it wasn't meant to be.
Not everybody's cut out for fame.
I'm good on the business end."
Marissa winked at Merc, brushing her hand
on his knee.

"Well . . . you're happy, right?"
Dali whispered, so soft
I almost missed it.

But Marissa bolted up from the sofa,
leaving Dali's question
hovering in the air.

"Follow me, girls. Merc's got something to show you."

"SURPRISE!!! HAPPY BIRTHDAY, DENVER!"

a crowd of cheering people shouted
soon as we reached the patio
decorated with
balloons,
streamers,
confetti,
cake,
presents,
the WORKS!

I scanned the faces
in the crowd,
most unfamiliar,
but some definitely not . . .
like
Lil' Mega
and
DJ Syncere
and
every! single! member!
of B-Unit!

A party
of epic proportions
with the stars!

I ugly-cried,
Dali jump-hugging me,
eyes all glistening.

"You knew about this, Dali?
But my birthday isn't until—"

> "Tomorrow?" Merc said, hugging both of us,
> Papa-bear style.
>> And for a moment,
>> I ached for family, for home,
>> until I remembered how empty ~~it~~ we were
>> for so long.

"Don't worry, Denver, you ain't seen nothing yet."

sipping champagne
with celebrities
to celebrate
the arrival,
the unfurling,
of
US,
the adulting
of
ME.

Fine cuisine,
hip-hop,
R&B,
OUR SONGS(!!!)
blasting,
me and Dali
losing our freaking minds!

Sun setting,
moon creeping,
mind made up
I was NEVER going back to Shohola,

drowned my whole self
in spirits of every color:

one shot
two shots
three shots
FLOOR!

DAY TWO, MY ACTUAL BIRTHDAY

Head   spinning,
sun   blinding,
pain   building,
gut   releasing,

every!
single!
thing!

my lips had touched
the night before.

(no monster period that time tho)
(and also . . . no Dali)

ELEVEN P.M.

I tossed and turned,
in the dark,
loneliness and
dreams taking root.

        I saw myself,
        so clear,
        two feet planted on the floor,
        rushing out the door,
        dashing down the hall

The walls were long
winding,
bending,
emotions sending
me on a
tailspin

        I grasped at each doorknob,
        door after door,
        each one
        locked, locked, locked
        some more

It was too dark,
too quiet back in that massive suite
and I needed someone,
anyone,
a taste of home.

        A ghost appeared
        a transparent image
        that morphed into
        a mindfuck on repeat
        First Ma
            then Shak
                then Gwen
                   then you, Papi

And finally, Dali,
playing hide-and-go-seek
as I chased her
to the farthest room
at the end of the hall

I placed my hand on the lever
and clicked it open

Candles lit,
                a smoky stench,
ganja hovering
                like a cloud,
                two lovers intertwined,
                completely unaware of my presence,
                lips pressed into parts I'd yet explored.

It wasn't Dali.
Nor Marissa.
Or Merc.
Or anyone I'd ever seen before.
                            One caught sight of me,
                            rapture on pause.
                            "Bounce yo!" someone shouted.

I turned on my heels, hauled ass,
landing smack-dab
against a giant teddy bear,
in human form

                "What are you doing outta your room, Denver?"
                Meat whispered,
                his breath a combination of peppermint and heat.

"I . . . I . . . was looking for Dali."
My voice cracked.
"Who was that back there?"

                Meat placed his hand on my shoulder,
                walking us both forward,
                leaving my question unanswered.

We reached my door.
"Merc wants you focused, Denver.
So try and rest. He's got a lotta
plans for you coming up. You'll see him in a few days."

"Days?" My throat felt raw.
"Where is he? Is Dali with him?
Answer me!"

But he didn't.
He closed my door, locked it with a key, and whispered, "I'm sorry."
That's when I knew I wasn't dreaming at all.

ONCE UPON A BIRTHDAY,

there was
cake (red velvet)
and candles (ages 1–9)
and
family
and
kompa music
and careers on pause
least for that day,
sometimes longer.
   But that all stopped
   many moons ago,
   leaving me
   to start traditions of my own,
   with my girls.

Tonight brought me back
to the memory
of forgotten birthdays.
    No need
    for codes to
    unlock phones,
    to check for texts, calls,
    a message or two,
    because
    time told the real truth
Pretty sure I stopped mattering
to y'all
a long time ago.
    Yet, other thoughts
    arose, unshakable:
     Was this the surprise Merc had for me?
     Birthday turnup with a side of isolation?
     Did Dali forget about me, too?

I undressed myself in the bathroom,
tried to rinse it all off
but there wasn't enough
soap in the world
to wash away
the questions
that remained
three layers deep
beneath my skin.

Day Three: Makeover

> Before the sun
> kissed the sky,
> Marissa tapped on
> my bedroom door.

> "Rise and shine, Denver."
> Her voice,
> surprisingly syrupy sweet.
>> "Is Merc back yet? I need to talk to him!
>> What's with Meat locking my door? And where's Dali?"
>> I hated how desperate I sounded.

> "You'll see everyone soon enough.
> Merc really wants you working hard
> on yourself. Even if that means staying in your room.
> Separation breeds focus, remember?
> Now get up, let's get you all the way
> together. Starting with this tragedy . . ."

> Marissa grabbed a thick chunk
> of my hair,
> grimacing when her fingers got stuck
> halfway through.
>> "This needs work, sis! Get dressed and meet
>> me in the salon in ten."
>> And then she bounced.

> Two hours later . . .

> Every hair follicle,
> from the crown to the kitchen,
> Marissa braided into submission
> hella-long extensions,
> all silky-n-smooth,
> stared at my reflection,
> like
> *New hair,*
> *who dis?*
>> When she was all done,
>> Marissa snapped her fingers.
>> "Yas! Now this, honey, is a *lewk*!"
>>> I liked it and all.
>>> Woulda liked it better if Dali was there to see it.

TEXTS ON MY OLD PHONE I DIDN'T SEE

August 14, 3:01 a.m.

Gwen: Ma and Papi called on your birthday and the next night, too. What's our next move?

Gwen: Denny, you there?

Day Four: still no Dali

But there was this . . .

A six a.m.,
Listerine-spiced
SHOUT:

"Wake up, superstar!"
Merc hovered over me,
jolting me outta my sleep
and I just about tackled him to the floor.
"Looks like somebody missed me," he said.

And I hit him with questions, rapid fire.
"How come I haven't seen Dali?
Or much of you, for that matter?
Why aren't we recording music?"

"Whoa, slow down! Say Say's fine.
I just took her on a little trip is all."

And something about that felt like,
I don't know . . . a threat? A game.

"Without me? Where? Why?"
Each question a siren, sounding off
inside of me.

Merc threw some extra honey in his voice.
"I'll let you see her soon, but first, put this on."

Then he handed me a pair of Nikes, some yoga pants,
and a T-shirt.

"Come downstairs. I got somebody I want you to meet."

AHMED RAKIM:

cut-up,
ripped-up,
veined-up,
muscle of a man,
aka personal trainer to the stars.

Hired by
Merc
to mold me
into someone
I wouldn't recognize
come the dawn
of the New Year.

His words,
not mine.

stretched to
the end of
God-knows-where.

Trees hovered.
Sun hid.
Nikes laced tight.
I hadn't been outside in days.

"It's so quiet out here," I said
to Ahmed.

"Better be.
Merc's nearest neighbor
is over a mile away."

Geez.
And I thought our crib
in Shohola was bad!

Ahmed blew his whistle.
"Buckle up, Denver.
Time to put in that work."

Merc winked at me
and then disappeared
inside the house.

WANNA KNOW WHAT PAIN IS?

Pain is . . .

running the entirety
of Merc's campus-sized
grounds,
not once,
but twice
while Ahmed drill-sergeant-yelled,
and Meat hung in the shadows,
half watching,
half glued to his phone.

Pain is . . .
pushing,
grunting,
while picturing yourself
singing for thousands of fans

Pain is . . .
squatting
through muscles
hidden beneath
cushions of the flesh
that needed
smoothing out . . .

a few pounds
here,
a few inches there
to snatch the
lady lumps

to a size
suitable
for TV,
magazines,
the
WORLD.

Did I like it?
Negative.

I call bullshit on the whole
notion that less is best.
But if having a certain type of body
was gonna make my voice heard,
then I had to make it do what it do.

ALL MY LIFE

I'd been told a
thing or two
'bout this body—
too thick for Shohola guys,
just right for Caribbean eyes—

See 'cause where
my people came from,
big bodies
on small islands
were a stamp of wealth,
prosperity,
success

But to level up to that grand stage
it's funny how I had to shed
parts of myself,
school,
       family,
              friends,
and now this body.

A loss for a win,
of sorts,

the cost of fame
was expensive AF.
              And I'd only just begun
              paying off my debts.

LIFE AT CASA DE MERCURY

became a ~~endless~~
~~repetitive~~
necessary routine
of six a.m. workouts

nasty-ass,
bland-ass
egg whites,
turkey burgers,
spinach

served by silent employees
—a new one, each time—
who wouldn't even look me in the eye

Me eating meals by my damn self,
or worse, with Marissa hovering

And sometimes . . .
No food at all.

No songs recorded,
no beats swimming through
headphoned ears.

Only new lyrics written,
guitar chords played
in the corner of my room.

And still NO DALI.

MORE QUESTIONS

"Are you playing some sick game
that I can't see Dali or record
until I fit some kinda model image?

"When can I call my sister?
My parents?

"Because
when they figure out
I'm *gone gone*,
they gonna beat my ass.
Twice."

Responses

"It's important that we're careful how
we reach out to your folks.
And you've done so good, baby gurl,
being patient and disciplined.
How 'bout tonight we
finally make some magic?"

Those words tumbled
off Merc's lips like sap
slow-rolling
down the bark of a tree.

TEXT FROM MY OLD PHONE I DIDN'T SEE

August 20, 8:48 p.m.

Gwen: Denny, call me ASAP. THEY KNOW.

Finally!

Merc brought Dali to my suite.
A reunion that
started with
a laugh, a hug,
a lift, a burst
of home.

        "Don't ever leave me like that again!"
        And I said that with one eye on Dali, the other
        aimed at Merc. "Where have you been?"

"Château Élan."
Dali spoke in a fake-ass
French accent.
Fireworks sprang in my chest.

        "You left the country?" I tried to rein it in,
        but damn.

Merc laughed.
"Nah, baby gurl, it's a resort,
with a state-of-the-art spa,
here in Georgia."
        But that didn't help. One bit.
        Especially since I was here
        all this time. Alone.

"I got a makeover, like you.
If you think my hair is short here,
you should see the rest of me.
I have, like, zero body hair now." She giggled.
"Oh, and I got my teeth done.
See? Ta dah!" Dali flashed
a braceless grill.

Dali's hair,
once cascading
like dark waterfalls down her back,
now barely touched
the tips of her ears

A spiky,
choppy,
badass
blond of a girl,

complete
with a silver ball
pierced through
a swollen tongue—
that had never
existed before.

                              "You stayed there? At the resort?"

"Well . . . yeah."
                              "Together?"

"Whoa!" Merc cut in
before she could answer.
"Slow down, baby gurl.
No, not at all."

Dali and I stood,
eyes locked on each other,
pieces of us both
slowly drifting,
changing.
"Look at *your* hair."
Dali ran her fingers through it.

"So pretty!"

Merc coughed.
"Should I leave or something?"

                              And I swear, right there,
                              I wanted to kick Merc out my room
                              and lock the door.

                              Instead, Dali laughed it off,
                              like that look and that touch
                              didn't even matter.

                    This is the spell Dali cast on me:
                    the ability to drink me in,
                    and spill me out at will.

I'd played her game
for years,
but a tiny voice inside wondered
Is she the only one playing me?

A look . . .
Unforgettable

> "I'm just trying to get you two to *look* like a unit."
> Merc grazed his hand across my waist.
> "See, baby gurl, you're getting there. Keep it up!"

A sound . . .
Iconic

> "When I'm done with you, folks will be calling
> Untouched living LEGENDS!"

And speaking of sound . . .
The time had come to work on ours.

> "Say Say, Baby Gurl,
> I wrote a new joint for y'all.
> Now let's put in that work!"

Relief
washed over me.

She was back.
So was he.
And together, that felt like

H
O
M
E

I think.

                    Really, I couldn't think
of any other way
to describe Merc's studio.
You would've loved it, Papi!

State-of-the-art
keyboards,
mics,
soundproof walls,
digital converters,
amps . . .

a secret,
hidden
paradise
to sing . . .

                              "Alone."
I felt the whole planet
pause on its axis when he said that.

"If Denver records by herself,
then where do I come in?"

But Merc ignored Dali's question.
Just pointed a wordless finger
at the black leather couch.

Handed me a sheet of lyrics,
had Meat lead me to the booth
empty,
confused . . .
solo.

WHAT BECOMES

of a voice
muted
far too long?

                     I'll tell you what . . .

mine turned into spiced air.
A welcome blend
of hushed tones,
belted riffs
over C minor chords,
blasting through
glass enclosures
soaring,
floating,
landing
next to

two brown eyes
that refused
to connect with my own.

                  Two takes

          was all it took
to record "Just Breathe."

And Dali refused
to look at me the entire time.

                        "That's a wrap!
                 Did you hear that, Say Say?
            That sound that came out
                     of Denver?
                        New?
                       Fresh?
                    Hungry?

            You ain't hungry enough.
                       Yet."

I left the booth,
joined Dali on the couch,
whispering, "Olive juice. Next time."

She pulled away and whispered back,
"It's all good."
(Was it though?)

Our (my?) session ended

in a reward—for both of us—
though I'm not sure you could call it that.

Because we both knew what was waiting
on the other end of the receiver
was anything but a prize.

Subject: Tía Esme
Dominican aunties be like:

"¡Muchacha de mierda!
Tú te estás volviendo loca, eh?!
¡Coño!"

With a side of:

"Cuídate.
Te quiero.
Mi amor, I don't want to stop you from your dreams."

And a promise from Dali to put out the fire:

"I'll be careful. I love you, too, Mami."

Subject: Ma and Papi
(yelled in the key of WTF)

"Where the HELL are you, Denver?
And don't lie because we already
spoke to Shak and Gwen!"

UGH!
Traitors, número uno and dos.
But was it wrong that I smiled through the threats?
Was it wrong I was happy that . . .

Y'all were home.
Together.
For once.
Missing ME?

You didn't see it yet,
but my leaving,
my journey,
had already started to fix us.
But my words meant nothing, apparently.

You:
"If you're not home by tomorrow night,
I'm calling the cops on that sick pervert
for kidnapping you."

Ma:
"It's gonna get ugly real fast, Denver."

Me:
"Kidnapping? Dramatic much?
He's a musician, Papi, like—"

But YOU hung up,
leaving my words
harmonizing with the dial tone.

"Can they do that?" I asked.
According to Merc, y'all *could try*.
But it wouldn't do much.

Because
his lawyer told him that
WE chose to leave home.

Merc didn't force us (true)
And he didn't threaten us (also true)
Plus, we were FINE!
So, it was all good.

Not everyone needed to be
close to their family . . .

or their friends.

Success came with sacrifice,
just like Merc said.

Weight: 8 lbs down
Breakfast: Roasted oxygen
Today's workout with Ahmed: Cardio (aka hell)

                    Around the big brick house

on Pristine Road,
Ahmed and I jogged

and I thought about Dali,
like always

Same house and yet
two different corners
of the world

I ran past
a pond
with some ducks,

a green forest
full of blood flowers,

a row of trees bearing
red-cheeked fruit,
and behind it,

a metal gate
with a big ole hole . . .
begging for repair.

And for a split second,
I pictured myself
running through it,
if for nothing else
to see what existed outside
La Casa de Merc,
the place I'd been trapped in all month.

But who was I kidding?
Every~~thing~~ one I needed
was right in that house.

Ahmed thought otherwise though.
"There's a whole world of opportunities
outside of this place,
but I'll take what I can get . . . for now."
He winked.
But I just rolled my eyes.
I didn't have time for small thinking.
Not then, not ever.

Eleven thirty p.m.

A revolving swirl
of red and blue
poured through my window,
awakening me
from my sleep.
A call from Merc on my phone:

"Get dressed.
Grab your wallet.
Meet me downstairs.
Put a smile on your face."

There was
a double-entry
set of steps,
each leading
to a different wing of the house.

To the right,
my wing.
To the left,
Dali's.

Our rooms
separated by
long hallways,
bedroom doors,
security
guarding
us like precious jewels.

But on that night,
no one was up there,
from what I could tell.
Not Marissa, not Meat,
or any other zip-lipped servant.

We met at the top of the stairs
before going down,
darkness enveloping us.
I wanted to lace my fingers in hers,
but it was the first time I felt
unsure of where things stood.

"Do you know what's going on?" I whispered.

"Got no clue," Dali whispered back,
wrapping her arm around mine.
"I miss you, chica. That part I know."

"Me too. I can barely sleep at night."
I stuttered over my words.

Under the cover of darkness,
Dali pulled me in
lips on tongue
like ocean waves,
crashing against the shore.

    "Ay yo!" Merc screamed from below.
    "What's taking so long?"

We released ourselves,
walking separately down the steps
just as Merc opened the front door.

"Officer Parsons, Atlanta Police Department."
One hand flashed his badge,
the other propped on top
of his gun belt.

    "Is something wrong, sir?" Merc asked.

    "Here to do a welfare check
    for Denver Lee Lafleur.
    Mind if we take a look around?"

Two policemen—
Officers Parsons and Anderson—
stepped into the grand foyer.

Parsons, with a face of stone.
Anderson, on the other hand,
had the swivel neck going,
big ole smile across his face,
like he ain't never seen
Swarovski crystal chandeliers before.

    "We received a call from a Captain Antoine Lafleur
    claiming that you, Mr. Ellis, were holding his daughter
    against her will."

And I was surprised for a moment
that it was you, Papi, not Ma.
Guess all I had to do to get your

attention was leave, which made sense.
You certainly had ours when you dipped off.

I realized everyone was looking at me,
waiting for an answer.

"That's not true!" I said. "My father is lying!"

                    "How old are you, miss?"
"Eighteen."
I flashed my driver's license,
my entire body brimming with heat.

                    "Looks like you just had a birthday?"
"Yes, sir." I nodded.
                    "And you are?" Parsons pointed to Dali.

But before she could answer,
Merc whipped out our contracts:
"These ladies are my recording artists."
Parsons scanned the papers,
turned his back to Merc,
like this wasn't his house,
and whispered in my face,

                    "Can you state with certainty
                    that you are in no danger?"

"Yes, Officer."
                    "And you left Pennsylvania of your own will?"

"Absolutely.
I could play you some of our music,
if you like? We're even going—"

                    Merc cleared his throat,
                        eyes morphed into red lasers.
Officer Parsons's radio beeped.
                    "Going to?"

"Nowhere . . . Officer," I said, staring at Merc.

Officer Parsons paused,
as if he waited for me to say more,
then lifted the radio to his lips,
                    "All clear,"

and slapped it back on his belt.

"Given Miss Lafleur's age,
and own admission,
we have no cause to pursue
further action.
We'll report back to the parents
that she is safe and in good health,
despite their wishes that she return home."

Officer Parsons pulled
his contact card from his back pocket
and then handed it to me.

             "In case you change your mind, young lady."
"I won't," I said.
But I slipped it in my robe anyway.

             Officer Parsons
                  shook Merc's hand
                       and headed to his car.

Anderson lingered
just enough so
Parsons didn't see
him hand Merc a
blank sheet of paper:
             "Can I get your autograph for my daughters?"

FOUR THINGS I LEARNED THAT NIGHT

1. You wanted me home.
2. But on what terms? Yours? Or mine?
3. And I wasn't sure how I felt. Happy you missed me? Disrespected? Both?
4. So because of that, I would stay in Atlanta. For me. This was my life, my dreams.

     Still,
             the reality of it all
                   was enough to send
                       my feet flying,
                              crying all the way upstairs.

BACK IN MY ROOM,

the mirror
reflected the whole
mess of me

satin bonnet
sliding down
swollen curls,

white-hot tears
against
crimson cheeks,

a tornado of a girl
dipped in deep thought

*When would my dreams
ever be good enough?*

A knock at my door

"May I come in?"
There was a tenderness in Merc's voice,
like soft jazz at midnight.
"Dali thought you might
need some company."

I didn't want
to be seen like that.
Hair, face
toe' up,
stained with rage.
Bones all exposed.
But Dali knew.
I didn't want to be left alone.

Dali came in first,
Merc followed.

"I'm so sorry, Denver," Merc said.
"I know that was probably scary for you."

He pulled us both close to him,
our faces nestling in the cushion of his chest.

He reminded me
to breathe through every sob.

"I went through this when I left home, too."
Merc handed me a bottle of water.

Slid a blue pill
onto my nightstand.
"In case you want to take the edge off."

But before I could do anything,
Dali flinched next to me, and then chirped,
"I'll take it!" and snatched it so quick,
popped it in her mouth
and swallowed,
no water needed.

"Damn girl," I half chuckled,
Dali's theatrics pulling me
out of the moment.

"Sorry." Dali smiled sweet, more at Merc than me.
"But tonight was just stressful."

"That's cool," I said.
"I didn't want it anyway."

"Suit yourselves." Merc shrugged.
"Say Say, you can stay with her
for a few minutes, but then
head back to your wing."

Merc flicked the lights,
and shut the door behind him.

I grabbed the bottle,
gulped all of it down,
and fell into Dali's embrace.

WATER

life-giving,
soul-filling,
cool,
magic,
washing away
tears,
dreams,
fears.

Blue eye, brown eye
part earth, part ocean
drifted away
arms,
legs,
mind
became
weightless

Twilight
and memory
turned
endless . . .

NINTH GRADE,

                             cutting eighth period,
                                   hanging out,
         hidden room
in the school basement.

                                One   touch,
                                one   kiss
                                            split us
                                in   two

                  "I'm not . . . like that."

And I whispered back,
"Pffft, me neither."

And it was true.
Least I thought.

What was the point
of labels anyway?

~~I~~ *We* tried to forget that day,
but trying was like
begging the moon
to not show its face.

My bed was empty, cold.
Dali gone,
disappeared in the middle of the night.

Ghosted on me
like some kinda hookup
gone wrong.
Did she want to leave?

That room,
that bed,
never lonelier.

As I stood and walked
to my window

Officer Parsons's card
fell out of my robe,
wedging itself
in a crack of wooden floor.

Was that you again, universe?
Some kinda sign?

The weight of my foot,
loosening the wood even more.

Big ole
brand-new-looking house
with a floorboard
like a removable puzzle piece.

I left the card right there,
let it fall between the cracks,

went to my bathroom,
washed away the stains of
cops banging on the door,
the pot of trouble you and Ma
stirred up.

I dried my face and headed out my bedroom,
but Meat was there,
leaning back in a chair.
Dude was everywhere.

"Good morning, Denver."
He stood up soon as he saw me.
"Ready for breakfast?"
"Bro, I'm next-level hangry."
We both chuckled.

I walked down the stairs,
through the halls,
through the kitchen
Meat trailing my every step,
until I reached the double doors
that led to the patio in front of the pool.

Dali was already there
dressed in a white robe, white towel
wrapped around her ice-blond hair.

The maid served me my plate—
two celery sticks and water.
On the rocks.
I wanted to say thank you,
but I knew she wouldn't respond.
It's like Merc had a revolving assortment
of staff, mouths on mute at all times.

Meanwhile she piled Dali's
and Meat's plates with pancakes and thick bacon.

Marissa sauntered
through the French doors,
beckoning. "Merc, I need you for a sec."

Soon as that man turned his back,

Dali, smile like the devil,
raised a finger to her lips
darted her eyes at Meat and whispered
shhhhhh

passed me a piece of salty,
greasy, crunchy slice of heaven.
I slid it between my lips,
rolled my eyes all around in rapturous delight
Meat chuckled,
"Y'all are hilarious!"

Chewed it up hella quick
before Merc saw

"Special announcement!" He clapped
his way back to the patio,
ending my bacony bliss
in a hurried swallow.

"I think you ladies are ready
to hit the road with me . . .
Next Saturday."

And me and Dali LOST IT!

Jumping up and down,
almost knocking over our food,
hands clasped real tight.

"Omg, Dali, stage lights,
fans screaming! We did it!"

"Together."
Dali folded her
whole self into me.

> "There's just one little thing
> I have to change."
> Merc sat back down,
> pierced his pancakes
> fork and knife,
took in a big bite.

"And, Say Say, you ain't gonna like it,
but it is what it is."

DEFINITION OF UNDERSTUDY:

As in
Substitute

As in
Fill-in for Denver, in case her voice needs a rest

As in
"Maybe we'll need your vocals, Say Say.
We probably won't, on this tour.
But don't worry . . .
I'ma keep you busy."

Dali's scream?
Guttural.

Her words?
A staccato of arrows,
      darting
without   destination.

"What about me?
You PROMISED, Merc!"

"Be patient.
You just need a little more practice.
Denver's ready . . .
right now."

Patio chair
tossed to the ground.
Meat reached for her,
     "Calm down, Dalisay,"
     his words, gentle,

but Dali wasn't trying to hear it.
Bare feet stomped on pavement
legs flew through the kitchen doors,

utensils dropped
next to the chair,
I chased the wind of her wings.
"Dali, hold up!"
I grabbed hold of her arm
before she reached the stairs,
her robe slipping off one shoulder,
revealing a small blue-purple bruise.

"What happened to you?"

Dali yanked away from me
as though my own hand was diseased.

                    "Hit myself on the stupid closet. It's nothing."

"Hey, I'll talk to Merc.
Convince him to let you sing.
I don't wanna do this without you."

                    "I don't need your favors, Denver."

Her words left
a trail of fire and ice
on the steps.

                              There was a tightness

                    working its way
from hair follicles
                    to toenails.

I did not want this.
I did not want this.
I did not want this.
(Not like this.)
                         "She'll get over it."

Merc strolled in
like World War III
didn't just pop off.

"You need to fix this NOW!
I don't wanna sing without Dali!"
I screamed straight at the
gray dawn of Merc's eyes.

He licked his lips,
smirk growing
from zero to a hundred.

Veiny hands wrapped
around my arms,
soft at first,
but then hard to the point
my blood stopped flowing.

                              "I'm not putting in all this
                              money, time, and effort

to be dealing with Say Say's
drama or yours!"

I yanked away
from his hardened grip,
the print of his fingers
remained
reddened
beneath my skin.

A sudden chill
filled that whole room.

"I'm sorry, Denver.
I didn't mean to . . ."

"Don't ever grab me like that again, Merc!"
I choked it out, and it took all my courage
to draw the line with the very person
who controlled my future.

"I know. I don't know what got into me.
I just believe in you so much.
I want the best for you.
We good?"

I nodded hesitantly through his honey-coated words.

"That's my gurl.
Now, meet me in the studio in ten.
Need you to link up with the other background singers.
It's gonna be a long week."

SHARMAINE AND ALTHEA

powerhouse,
church-bred,
Atlanta-born
voices from heaven.

Every day and night,
we practiced background
to all the songs in
Merc's catalog.

We sang through
every note,
every harmony

Mine, folded into theirs
like a blanket
on a cold winter's day

But that's all we did together though.
Sing.
And when I tried to
strike up a convo,
they hit me with
            "Merc said we're here to work.
            Not make friends."

Which sent a chill
slowly growing inside

Only thing that coulda
fixed that
was if I had Dali
and that skin-deep soprano
melting right along with mine.

SATURDAY, AUGUST 31

Weight: 13 lbs down
Breakfast: what is breakfast again?
Last workout with Ahmed before the tour: cardio, weights
(equal parts torture and hell)
Lunch: celery, ½ can tuna, sautéed tears

The afternoon rolled in

Four tour buses waited for us
at the edge of the driveway.

It was the first time I saw just
how tight Merc ran his operation

Backup singers and dancers,
all girls,
single file in front of
bus number four.

The band,
all guys,
lined up in front of the third bus.

The second bus was for the security team—
and me.

Dali, Merc, Marissa,
and management
rode on the lead bus.
Without me.

It's like Merc played Ping-Pong with us:
Who's the favorite today?

"Why can't I ride with you and Dali?"

I was all for discipline,
but life on the road
shoulda been a little fun, no?

"We'll swap midway through,"
Merc said.
"Gonna take some time to work on Dali's upper register.
You want her to sing with you eventually, right?"

The doors on the bus closed in my face.
Meat told me to make myself at home.

IN CASE YOU WERE WONDERING

what a tour bus looks like,
picture an apartment on wheels.

Inside:
a mini kitchen,
table with a cushioned bench
against double windows

a row of single beds,
six of 'em,
each with curtains for privacy

a small bathroom
with a small shower
and even smaller toilet
clearly not made
for humans,

and in the back,
Merc's private bedroom
always locked
whether he was in there or not.

RULES OF THE BUS

Rule #1: Each crew was to remain separate—
for focus, of course

Merc didn't need no one messing up his vibe
That focus was what made his show
Top notch
The best there ever was

Rule #2: Don't nobody talk to Dali or Denver

Rule #3: annnnnnd vice versa

SEPTEMBER

A new city each week

Nashville
  Charleston
Raleigh
  Richmond

Spotlights zoomed
on Merc

Dancers grinding
Band grooving

Me
Sharmaine
Althea

The perfect
soprano-alto-tenor blend
beneath
the bass of his
melodies

while Merc
was center stage
living his best life

That girl behind stage right,
off in the shadows?
That was Dali
  watching, watching, watching.

Two a.m.

Hunger pangs
ricocheted through my ribs,
up to my eyes, blasting
me awake.

In the bunks around me,
everyone
was snoring hella loud.

Outside my window
a crescent moon followed
the bus down I-95.

I got up
for the bathroom,
ran cool water on my face,
headed to the kitchen,
quietly poured half a can
of Pringles in my mouth,
saw the blue light blinking
laptop open, headphones attached,
crying out

Denver, come talk to me . . .

What was life
without checking
email,
Instagram,
text messages?

Hard at first,
easier as the weeks went by.

But that open screen
was like dangling a steak magnet
in front of greedy lips.

From: drlafleur@wemail.com
To: denverleexoxo@wemail.com
Cc: captainlafleur@wemail.com

September 10

Subject: Please come home, baby

Dearest Denver,

From the moment I felt your first kick inside my womb, I knew you were my special girl. Feisty. Fearless. You entered this world singing in the key of C sharp, so says your papi.

And when we laid eyes on you, all pink and wrinkly, one brown eye, one eye blue,
we made a vow. To love you down to your bones. To always be there, listen, support your dreams. To allow you to spread your wings, let you love how you choose, let you make mistakes along the way.

I think we may have failed you in our promise. Papi and I understand why you left. It's not your fault. We will take some of the blame. But your "music producer" is not without fault. The way he manipulated you into leaving has left us empty.

Mr. Ellis recently sent Esme a check for $5,000. His team contacted us as well to offer the same, but your father and I declined. We do not care about money. We care about your well-being.

It's not too late to come home, Denny.

Love,
Ma and Papi

PS: Attached is a gift from Papi.

PPS: I am worried for your mental and physical health.

I SLIPPED THE HEADPHONES ON

and clicked play

The video opened
and I heard Ma whisper,
"It's recording."

She tried her best to hold
the camera steady,
zooming in on
an image of hands
I knew all too well
                    fingernails begging for a trim
                    ashy-ass knuckles (you stay needing lotion, Papi)
                    and that ebony skin.

You sat at the piano in our basement,
the one you hadn't touched in years

From the very first chord
of Prelude in E Minor,
you
gutted me,
broke me,
tears warm
and thick,
falling in rapid succession.

The memory
of you both
lovingandleaving me
on repeat,
was enough
to make me click
STOP

Because that song
and that video
were like a heavy anchor
on the soul.

I suppose that's just
the way Chopin (*y'all*)
intended it to be.

GOOGLE TOLD ME

Three things:

1. I wasn't some victim.
2. It's not like Merc kidnapped me.
3. Even if I wanted to leave, I wasn't going nowhere. Not without Dali.

I had so much more to say to y'all
but all I could email back was:

I am not sick.
I am safe, I promise.
Now, please, just let me live.

LIKE AN OLD FRIEND,

Google and I reconnected once more.
Told me all the things
I already knew about Merc

Superstar
      Award-winning artist
Tour dates
      Collabos with the finest in the industry

Page after page
of all that was right
about the King of R&B.

It wasn't until I got
to page sixteen
that I stumbled on
a clickbait site with
that stupid article Shak sent.
Seriously, who even digs that far?

My next search, Marissa Avent,
produced an Instagram page,
six years ago, not a single post since.
A fresh-faced, messy-bunned Marissa,
pressing play on her iPod,
volume up on the instrumental track
for Merc's "Strawberry Lipstick."

The second she opened her mouth,
vocals set fire to my ears,
a gut-deep blend of
Lizzo-meets-Adele,

which begged the question . . .

*Why on earth would she give up singing
just to be Merc's personal assistant?*

I HEARD

                 a rustling coming from the bunk beds,
a planting of feet against the floor.

I cleared my history,
put the screen to sleep,
and dashed to the sink,
cup in hand
just in time to hear
                 "What're you doing up?"

It wasn't a lie
that I was thirsty—
both in the literal
and metaphorical.

Either way,
it was enough to
make Meat believe
that nothing more,
nothing less
took place in the dark.

SATURDAY, OCTOBER 12

Weight: 22.9 lbs down
Breakfast: we don't get down like that no mo'
Lunch: celery, tuna, crackers, air
Dinner: see lunch
Today's workout: Ain't nobody got time.

                    Life on the road was

practicing background vocals,
studio time after the show
till the wee hours of the morning,
while Dali looked and looked and
nothing else.

Life was me
questioning
the when,
the why,
the how much longer,
he would do my girl like that?
                    Though I never spoke up.

Life was Merc
honey-coated promising,
capturing special moments,
camcorder gripped in hand.

Life was shopping sprees,
clothes and jewels and kicks
to purchase the "forgetting"
of who I once was.

Life was being spotted by fans,
girls drooling at Merc's feet,
hard eye-rolling at me and Dali
as if *we* were in the way.

And sometimes life was
a nosy-ass TMZ cameraman,
in hot pursuit
as we walked back to the tour bus.

A SEARING QUESTION

"Merc, what do you have
to say about
the recent accusation
you are holding girls hostage?"

And you know me and my tongue
these teeth
this mouth
was never afraid of unleashing the heat!

"Look around, idiot!
Does it LOOK like any of us are hostages?
It's not 1821!
You got your centuries wrong, bruh!"

Merc started laughing,
still walking,
but didn't stop me,
so I kept going.

"I swear the media tries so HARD
to bring a Black man down!"

"I'm sorry, miss. And you are?"

"Denver.
Half of Untouched—remember that name."

"Lafleur?"

Legs on full stop. The whole crew, too.

"Excuse me?" I said.

"Any comment on the latest article in the *Buzz*?"

TMZ dude, paper in hand,
reached toward me,
too slow for Merc's swift snatch.
                    Merc laughed a laugh
that I couldn't quite read.

Part amused?
Part shocked?

"No comment."

Stuffed that paper in his pocket,
climbed on the bus,
as if those TMZ folks
never existed.

OH, THE SHADE!!!!!

But I was still standing there,
teeth gritted,
eyes rolling like
Y'all can keep it moving.

Dali yanked me by the arm
extinguishing the rest of the heat
I wanted to let out,
pulled me onto her bus,
just in time for the driver to close the door
and dip off.

"AY YO, SAY SAY!

Read that out loud for me."
Dali smoothed out the crumpled-up paper,
cleared her throat,
and began . . .

Written By: The Buzz Staff

SECOND SET OF PARENTS STEP FORWARD WITH ACCUSATIONS AGAINST SEAN "MERCURY" ELLIS

An article in the *Daily Gossip* featured an interview with parents who have asked to have their names withheld. After further investigation, it was found that the daughter is indeed safe and thriving as a valuable member of Mr. Ellis's Merc World Productions team.

A new report has cropped up, this time from a married couple out of Shohola, Pennsylvania. Dr. and Captain Lafleur claim their 18-year-old daughter, Denver, and her best friend (name withheld) left home and dropped out of school, under Mr. Ellis's influence.

"It is our belief that Sean Ellis has brainwashed our daughter," Captain Lafleur tells us. "Because of that, we are worried for her safety," the mother added.

Attempts to file kidnapping charges proved futile after Atlanta PD conducted a wellness check to verify that Ms. Lafleur was indeed safe. Ms. Lafleur left home in August to pursue her musical ambitions under Merc World Productions, and turned the legal age of eighteen shortly after her arrival. The parents claim they have not heard from their daughter since.

In response to these new allegations, a representative for Mr. Ellis stated: "The parents of both girls signed contracts, allowing Mr. Ellis to take them under his tutelage for the purpose of developing them into recording artists. Their relationship is professional. Further, both families have been compensated to assist with expenditures, though they have since repeatedly requested more money."

THERE'S A SAYING THAT GOES

where there's smoke,
there's fire.

Well, I was on the defense with that one.

Where there's smoke,
sometimes that's all it was.

A gray cloud of nothingness,
the truth lurking behind
just waiting for the smoke to clear.

your parents are starting to become a problem!"

That act with the TMZ folks—
the soft chuckle,
the "take the high road" demeanor
was just that—
an act.

The Merc inside the walls of that bus?
His mood slowly unraveling.

"I don't know why they did that,"
I said, leaving out
the part about
our email exchange a few weeks back.

I looked at Dali,
seated at the kitchen table,
literally folding into herself,
locking in all the secrets I'd shared with her:
that song I stole on my flash drive,
that email I sent,
that Google search.

The reality settled
that even though that *Buzz* article
was covered in lies,
there was one part that was true.

Dali's mom needed that money.
Every cent of it.

But mine didn't.
At all.
"Did my parents really try to stick you for coins?"

Merc looked at me,
like how dare I ask such a question?

"I told you how folks get, Denver.
How fame and money
make people change.
Like it or not,
even your own blood will
do whatever they can
to stop what you got growing.

                                        It's up to you to make a decision:
                                               You in or you out?"

Dali zapped me with those pleading eyes.
I couldn't turn back.
Not when I knew what was waiting for us.
Radio. Videos. Red carpets. *Fame.*

"What can I do to
kill the noise and get them off our backs?"

Merc finally smiled,
pulled me in for a hug
as Dali stared at us both,
finally exhaling a trapped breath.

                                        "You my little ride-or-die chick,
                                               aren't you, baby gurl?"

I nodded, eyes sealed,
safeguarding defiant tears.

                                        "I got a little project for both of
                                                       y'all."

IF MERC COULDA BEEN

anything in the world
other than world-famous,
legendary,
the best to ever
throw down on a beat,

he woulda been a director
and gave
Ava and Spike
a run for their money.

That iPhone,
that tripod,
those hands
blended together
like the perfect coverup.

The script was done—
he wrote, Dali and I memorized—

We looked like
a real-deal
singing duo,
matching black-and-silver outfits.

Our newest song
"Brand-New Me"
played low in the background,

lights on,
me and Dali
side by side in our seats,
quiet on set,
going live on Instagram
in three, two, one . . .

Interviewer (aka Meat, off camera, news reporter voice down pat): What would you like to say in response to your parents' accusations?

Me: As you can see, I'm fine.

Dali: We both are.

Meat: Why do you think your parents went to the media?

Me: Control.

Meat: How so?

Dali: That's what parents do sometimes. And I won't speak for Denver's parents. My mom, on the other hand, isn't that controlling. She didn't like that I left school and home, but I know that she understands why. This is a chance to make something of myself, to pull my family out of the situation we're in.

Meat: What do you want Merc's fans to know?

Me: That he is an incredible human being, an amazing musician, who puts other people first.

Dali: That's why he's taking all this time to help us grow as artists.

Meat: Do you think your parents are exploiting the situation for money?

Me: . . .

Meat: Denver?

Me: . . . I can't speak on that right—

Merc swiped his hand across his throat.
CUT!

COMMENTS I DID NOT SEE

275,953 views
MERC PROTÉGÉ BREAKS SILENCE AFTER HOSTAGE ACCUSATIONS.

View all 3,812 comments

Justbecool: Time to #MuteMerc. Seeing this headline creep up again on this dude.

_Markani4: Damn, even parents tryna stick you for your paper!

WeKangz: Anybody see the hand shadow, telling that poor girl to shut her mouth?

Ballershak: Praying for my sisters. Wake up @denverlee01 @dalisaybabe!

GwennieLafleur: @denverlee01 what is happening to you? You look emaciated and pale!! I'm taking the semester off and coming back home to help find you. Please, please call me! I promise I will answer.

Detroit, Michigan
The tour bus pulled behind
Little Caesars Arena.
My nerves?
a bubbling-hot mess
That feeling never got old.

Lines wrapped around the whole building
crowds huddled in epic proportions
I scanned the faces upon faces as we entered,
heard the chants,
the fans screaming Merc's name.

But then in the distance,
I saw a small
cluster of signs
held high in the air.

Venom spewing through
every painted red word:

Merc is a monster!
Merc is a predator!
#MuteMercNow

Merc wasn't perfect,
I knew that.

The isolation,
the separation,
of me,
Dali,
Us.

I hated how he
had me spoonfeed lies
about my own parents
on Instagram.
        But y'all lied first.
We weren't prey.
And he wasn't a monster.
Wasn't no hero either,
but who said we needed one?
                    There was a huddle
        in front of the double steel doors
Flashing lights

a whole chorus of voices
calling out Merc's name

Meat and a large security team
sandwiched us all in
singers, dancers, musicians,
claustrophobia settling in my bones

"Sha . . ."
A familiar voice,
drowned deep within the noise.
"Shashou?" I whipped myself around.

Heartbeat quickened,
I jumped up
scanning the crowd,
searching for hair,
thick and always piled
to the heavens.

When we were little
Gwen and I
would call each other
Shashou,
Haitian Creole for
my baby,
my sweetheart,
        Sha for short.

The huddle grew tighter
moved faster
among a sea of faces,
black, brown, and everything
in between,

double doors slammed fast
behind #TeamMerc.
                I ran to them,
                dropping the bags in my hand,
                Meat blocked my path.
                "Gonna need you to
                head to the dressing rooms, Denver."

"I think my sister's here.
Let me out," I begged.

But Meat just stood there
scrunching up his face.
"Does she work for *Billboard* magazine?"

"No." My eyes began to sting.
"Hollywood Edition? Vogue?"
"No." Sting turned to water.

"Then I doubt that was your sister.
Those people have media passes.
Now Merc needs you down in hair and makeup.
Show's starting soon."

Was I losing my mind?
I know what I heard.
Sha . . .

If it was Gwen,
she would
have tackled
herself through the crowd.

Yeah, that felt about right.
Plus, it couldn't have been my perfect sis.
She was studying abroad in Paris,
going on with her life, her dreams.

I grabbed my things,
and made my way downstairs,
told myself I had my
own dreams to chase.

Like Meat said,
we had a show to do.

back in June?
At the Prudential in Newark?
Three girls with
starlight in their eyes,
swooned
and swayed
and prayed
that they could
be up there
singing with Merc?

And remember that moment
he pulled Dali
from the stage,
serenaded her with
his signature song?

Fast-forward
four months.

As the bass thumped,
Merc jumped off the stage,
landing directly in front
of a girl,
cornrowed,
Merc's face plastered
on her red T-shirt,
faced stained with omg tears.

"What's your name and age?" Merc sang into the mic.
"Isabel Fadden! Old enough, ha!"

"Wanna sing with me?"
"OMGOMGOMG!!"

Merc grabbed
homegirl by the hand,
pulled her center stage,
and together they sang "Do Me"
while her friends went apeshit!

Homegirl sounded a HAWT MESS
as her body folded into Merc's,
lights dimmed low, curtains closed.
End of the show.

In our dressing room,

Dali paced the floor
like she missed an appointment or something.

"You okay, girl?"
            "What's taking him so long?"

"Who, Merc? Beats me."

            "Did you hear that girl? Wack-ass vocals!
            Teeth all jacked up? Toe'-up braids? Dancing with Merc?"

I laughed hard
'cause Lord knew
Dali was telling the truth.

"Who cares?
It's just an act anyway.
No different than
what he did with you the first night."

            Dali stopped pacing.
            Then she just busted out crying.

Thick tears,
rapid succession.

"Dali, what did I say?"
            "Just STOP!" she screamed at the top of her lungs.
"Stop what?"

Back pressed against the dressing room wall,
Dali slid down to the floor.

            "You don't get it.
            Everything works out for you, Denver.
            You write the songs, you perform background,
            and I just sit and watch. And I'm trying to be happy
            for you, I swear, but it's hard. And I hate myself
            for feeling this way."

I knelt down beside her.
Grazed my fingers through her spiky hair.

"He's gonna put you in the next show.
I can feel it, Dali."
            "Is that all you feel about Merc?"

My mouth twisted,
brain fogged up hella fast.

"I mean, he's kind to you, right?
He's never tried to . . ."

Silence took precedence
over unfinished sentences.

"Tried what?
Something fresh?"
—I could feel bile catch in my throat—
"Um, no. Why? Did he try
something with you?
Like that time he took
you to that resort . . ."

"No, no, no." Dali wiped the last of her tears,
nestled her head against my chest.

"I thought I saw Gwen tonight . . . well, *heard* her,"
I said, a hint of disappointment settling.

"Ain't she at some fancy French school?" Dali asked.

"Yeah." I choked out my response. "I was just tripping."

"I think I miss home, Denver."
"Me too."
The weight of those words
lived, breathed, grew
inside of me.

Saying it loud,
like Dali did,
split me open,
made me feel everything
I'd been trying not to.

I missed Brooklyn
I missed Ma
I missed YOU, Papi
I missed Gwen
I missed Shak

And Shohola—
a little bit.
"We'll visit soon," I said.

"First thing I'ma have Mami do
is make you some Dominican food.
Getting too flaca on me, girl."
Dali tapped my stomach,
only it didn't jiggle like it used to.

The thought of
Tía Esme's sancocho
with a side of avocado awakened my
whole spirit.
                        "You sure we'll go home again?" Dali asked.

"All celebrities visit
their old stomping grounds. Right?"
I winked.

But she didn't answer back.
Just stared at me
hella hypnotic
trapped me into
a push and pull
of yes and no

                        Lips touched,
                tongues intertwined,
memories sparked,

drowning deep,
hands folded,
melting,
blending,

into that thing
I (she? we?) always did,
but never spoke of
again
        and
                again

But . . .
a loud tap

rattled the door,
pulled us straight out.

"Time to roll!" Marissa yelled through
the crack, then slammed it.

Dali jumped up,
started grabbing her things fast.
"I can't do this anymore!"

I sat on the floor,
stunned for a second,
wanting to remind her

of who-kissed-who

And that all those other times
it wasn't me, Dali, it was . . .
you.

        Even though
        I never stopped her.

Was she ashamed of us?
Was I?
I think the answer was both
no and yes

Me and Dali
were the visual representation of
a question mark, in human form.

But the real question was . . .
Did I care?

I liked
the perfectly
imperfect
broken
hidden pieces of us.
And for me,
that was enough.

"I'm out!"
Dali bolted through the door.

               Running after her,
       I saw Merc walking past the buses,
       Panasonic in hand,
       Isabel with the fuc'd-up braids
       diva strutting for the camera.

       I swear groupies stayed thirsty.
       Ready at a moment's notice to give it up to Merc
       or anyone in his entourage.
       Glad me and Dali weren't like that.

Meat told everybody to keep walking,
but Dali slowed her stride
once she saw Merc,
cursed "I hate you, pendejo,"
clutched her stomach
and just let . . .

G
O
!!!

I started rubbing my hands
against her back, like mad.
                              "What's wrong with you, Dali?"
"Get off me, yo!"
She yanked away,
as if my touch was a disease.

Then she hunched over again
and kept going-going-going.
                    Merc's ass didn't even stop to help.
                    Instead he and that girl
                    made their way to the limo waiting.
                    "Ay yo, Marissa, make sure you clean that shit up!"

Limo doors slammed.
Merc sped off beneath a full moon.

BACK IN DALI'S HOTEL ROOM,

Meat poured a glass
of ginger ale
laid out saltine crackers
and a steaming Cup of Noodles.

"You gotta stay hydrated."
Meat tried to feed her,
but she didn't even flinch.

I ran cold water
over washcloths,
whispered *olive juice*
as I wiped her sweaty face,
but she wasn't having that either.

"I ate something bad.
I'll be better tomorrow.

Just leave me alone, both of you.
I don't need your fuc'n help!"

She sprang up from the chair,
led us to the door,
and slammed that shit
in both of our faces.

TEXTS I DID NOT SEE

October 17, 11:57 p.m.

Gwen: I get it. You're upset with me for ratting you out. But I'm not sorry for worrying about you. You didn't have to sic four bodyguards on me tonight. I just wanted to see you again. Make sure you're okay. We're falling apart without you, Denny. Please, just call me back.

The rising of the sun
brought a morning
I wasn't prepared for.

Three buses lined up
all set to head back to Atlanta
each crew with their own.
I recognized every face,

except the one I needed
to see the most.

"Let me talk to Dali,"
I told Merc.

"She left. You'll ride with me."

"What do you mean *left*?
Like to use the bathroom inside the hotel?
I can wait."

"Nah, more like adiós."

"She wouldn't do that," I said.

Though the memory
of her words
still rang fresh in my ear.

"But she's coming back, right?"

Merc shrugged.
"Doubt it.
She left you this note though."

Denver,

Do you. You were always the most talented one anyway.

I'm out.

Dali

"WHAT I TELL YOU?

> Not everyone is built for this.
> But you? You're a real one."

But I didn't *hear him* hear him,
because I was too busy
trying to form thoughts
into words.

> Dali woulda never up and left.
> Not without me.
> Not without a real goodbye.

And definitely
not with that trash-ass note.
Right?
. . . .

       (right.)

PART FOUR: LANDING

Monday, December 23
Lehigh Valley International Airport
Time: 10:35 a.m.
Final Destination: 41.325560° N, -74.808130° W

promises a safe landing,
but not a calm passage.

You used to always say that, Papi.
I thought it was your fancy pilot talk.

But now?
The message is like a stain I can't wash out.

I am home. (almost)
I am safe. (finally)
(thankyouthankyouthankyou)

LADIES & GENTLEMEN:

the temperature in Lehigh Valley, Pennsylvania,
will be a high of forty-seven degrees,
with a low of thirty-four degrees,
and partly cloudy skies.

We will arrive
in approximately
forty-five minutes.

We here at Spirit Airlines
would like to thank you
for flying with us today
and wish you and yours
happy holidays.

Flight attendants,
please prepare the cabin for landing.

I ONCE READ

that when a white-browed
sparrow weaver
begins to sing,
its partner joins in—
their duet in perfect tune.

I know you can't
hear me singing
from where you're seated, Papi,
but soon as we land,
I'll raise my voice
loud enough to harmonize
with yours.

And when we
get to our destination,
can you play
Prelude in E Minor
for me . . .
for old times' sake?

FRIDAY, OCTOBER 18

How Merc reacted to Dali dipping off:

A shrug
a hug

Silent ride
walk inside

The house
lights out

Like
        she
                never,
                        ever
                                mattered.

HOW I REACTED:

Two a.m.

I lay in bed
tears rolling,
biting down
on the pillow
to muffle words,
curses,
screams,
apologies.

I imagined her
next to me in the mass
of that lonely room.

Olive juice, Dali.
I'm glad I said it last night,
and I meant every word.

Even though she
didn't say it back
that time.

I'm sorry it wasn't enough
to keep her.

Maybe I was the one
who was never enough for Dali.

Was she with her family?
With mine?
Did they miss me?
Did she?

And Merc,
I know he never really saw Dali.
Not the way I did.

                                    I should have
spoken up,
said something,
anything
to make Merc see

that her voice
that gift

was just as good,
if not better,
than
(mine.)

A tap on my door
before he opened it
and walked in.
        "I can hear you all the way downstairs, Denver."

"I just need to talk to her.
You have to let me call her!
She's more important to me
than your stupid boot camp rules!"
I cried out.

        Those last words,
        a roundhouse kick to Merc's gut.
        His face hardened, but his words
        did the opposite.

"Okay, baby gurl.
You win."

Merc pulled out my phone,
and through my tearstained fingers,
I did everything I could to
catch a glimpse
of the digits
Merc typed
before he handed it to me.
        0-2-2-7
Got it.

Dali's number rang . . .
and rang . . .
into nothingness.
        "Why won't she answer?" I sobbed and sobbed.
        "Maybe she left her phone at the hotel?"

        I was uncontrollable now.
        Back convulsing,
        tears and snot merging as one.

"No, baby gurl, she's got her phone.
She just doesn't wanna talk to you.
Or me. You gotta let her go."

Letting go
was never an option.
How could he not see that?

"Denver, you're gonna cry
yourself into a fever.
Here take these."
            "What are they?"
"They'll take the edge off."

I thought back
to the night Dali took that pill
Merc offered.

            Strange as it sounds,
            I wanted to take them
            if for nothing else,
            to transport me back to that night
            of her, me, together in my bed.

I popped two pills in my mouth,
gulped down the large glass
of water he handed me,
praying it'd be enough to do enough.

"That's my girl."
Merc tucked me in,
just like Ma used to do
when me and Gwen were little.

He pulled the curtains open
so a patch of moonlight
poured through the window
and down on my face.

            "How am I supposed
            to do this without Dali?"

"That's easy," Merc said.

"Like every other solo artist.
One song,
one lyric at a time."

Solo
never
fit the image
I dreamed
for myself.

How was I supposed to be hopeful
when I felt
SO
LOW?

SOME

times
the
very
best
dreams
take
root
with
your
eyes
wide

O
P
E
N . . .

First day of third grade

backs pressed against
the playground wall.

Two new students
silently watched,
    children playing,
        world moving,
            barely existing.

Took in the wonders
of a world that was new to us:
Shohola, Pennsylvania.

Transported from different places:
me from Brooklyn,
and Dali,
from Dominican Republic.

Two boys—one scrawny, one tall
ran up to Dali.
"Say something in Mexican!"
Dali twisted her face, in classic WTF.

"Like tacos!"
the other one laughed.
            "I'm not Mexican. I'm from Santo Domingo."
            Dali's words barely
            broke through the playground noise.

"What'd she say? Burrito and finito?"
Skinny ass teased.
Tall one laughed,
like it was the greatest
joke ever told.

Little did they know,
when you were from Brooklyn,
iron knuckles cracked easily on loose lips,
induced racist white boy tears,
made feet scatter like roaches.

Some friendships

are born from
coincidence,
knuckle sandwiches,
and
school suspension.
(with a side of música)

That was the beginning
of the story of
us.

TEXTS I SNUCK FROM MY UNLOCKED PHONE

October 19, 1:02 p.m.

Me: I know you're coming back here, so stop overreacting. I'm waiting.

Dali:

October 22, 4:29 p.m.

Me: I'm sorry. Can you forgive me? I'm still here, waiting for you.

Dali:

October 26, 2:36 a.m.

Me: I can't stay here any longer. Not without you. I'm coming home.

October 26, 2:37 a.m.

Dali: Don't.

OCTOBER 26, 2:38 A.M.

I   dialed
and   dialed
and   dialed
breath   paused.

                    It   rang
                    and   rang
                    and   rang
                    calls   ignored.

I   paced
and   paced
and   paced

until she left me
no choice.

          Packed my bags,
          under the cover of darkness.
          Told myself,
          Tomorrow, I'm going home.

First, the smell
woke me up.

A mixture of
meat, heat, and mildew.

Then it was the sound,
heavy, constant
panting.

I opened my eyes,
and staring back at me?

A little,
happy
bundle of fur,
licking,
slurping
my face
like an ice cream cone.

"You got a puppy?"

I wasn't sure who was
smiling more,
Merc or the dog.

> "You mean YOU got a puppy.
> I couldn't watch you moping
> around here another day.
> Thought this little guy
> would cheer you up."

"Omg, thank you! What is he?"

> "An Otterhound,
> rare British breed,
> can get up to 125 pounds.
> Sucka cost a grip, too,
> so you better like him."

I wrapped my arms
around that ball of fluff so tight,
it almost made me forget about my plan.

"Oh, I love him! I think I'll call him . . .
Fluffy!"

"Nah, too fairy-tale.
How 'bout Chance?
Something to describe the journey,
ya know?"

Merc stayed dropping wisdom.

"Yeah, Chance.
That's perfect."

Merc placed Chance's leash
on my nightstand,
started for the bedroom door.

"Get dressed and meet me in the studio.
I got another surprise for you."

"Merc, we should talk
about Dali . . .
I need to go—"

"Trust me, baby gurl."
Merc hit me with a
wink-smile-nod three piece.
"You wanna see this."

HERE WERE THE THOUGHTS THAT SWIRLED IN MY HEAD:

1. Dali came back.
2. Dali came back.
3. Dali came back.
4. FOR ME!

I washed my face.
I brushed my teeth.
I combed my hair.
I got dressed.

I
never
ran
so
fast
in
my
life
!!!

Down the steps,
past the kitchen,
past the library,
past the
gym
     spa
         salon

the music boomed
    LOUDER
        stronger.

Our songs,
Untouched,
masterfully retouched,
trumpets blazing,
harmonies grazing
the inner pieces of me.

I heard that
classic Denver-Dali
blend
as I turned the doorknob,
swung open the studio door,

screamed over the bass,
"I knew you'd bring dat ass back, chiiii . . . ca!"

Two leather chairs
swiveled around,

Merc on the left, camcorder in hand,
and NOT DALI on the right.

Instead,
a candy-lip-coated,
Timberland-wearing,
finger snapping
Nayeli Terron.

Aka
Queen Yeli
Aka
female rapper
who knocked
Cardi B off
the #1 Billboard spot

not once,
but four times . . .
this year!

I don't remember
who spoke first
but that smile
and that hug
sucked up
every word
that raced through my mind.

Merc recorded that whole moment,
my reaction, that squeal,
Queen Yeli laying it on
hella thick . . .

"So nice to meet you, Denver!
Your vocals are crazy dope!
We definitely gonna have to collabo!
When I get back from my European tour fo' sho!
I got the perfect song for us!
You'll still be here in December, right?"

Two hours spent
chilling in the studio

with the hottest artist
on the charts,
she took selfies of the two of us
making kissy faces, tagged my name
and posted on Instagram for
the WHOLE world to see us flexin'!

                    Every passing second
                    felt like
        freedom
            amnesia
      bliss
           a middle finger to the one
           who called this dream of mine *little*.

                        After Queen Yeli left,
                  Merc and I took a walk around
              the grounds of his massive property,

        the Atlanta sun
        playing coy behind thick clouds.
        At the pond,

we tossed food at the fish
as autumn leaves
drifted in the breeze.

        "You believe in fate, baby gurl?" Merc pointed to
        the heavens.
"Yeah, I do."

        "Denver, what we got, our music, this empire
        we're building? That's just for us. Nobody else. Time
        to start cutting folks off, you feel me."
I felt something, all right.
Equal parts
Yes-and-no-and-maybe.

        "Now, where'd you wanna go again, Denver?"

I tipped my face to the sky,
surrendered my voice to the wind.
"Nowhere, Merc."

(I wasn't going nowhere at all.)

I tucked away my exit strategy,
remembering Dali's text.
She didn't want me around, no how.

        So why leave,
        when the chance to fly

was right there in Atlanta?
(and beyond)

(Almost) back to normal,
Merc ramped up my schedule again,
minus the workouts with Ahmed,
—*Homeboy don't match our vision*, Merc said—
We recorded music on repeat,
hit up the hottest clubs
and hookah lounges at night.

An added bonus,
taking Chance for walks
around the property,
just nowhere near
the hole in the fence
by the peach trees.

Merc cautioned me
to keep away from the front gates, too.
Why?

Because on the
other side,
~~paparazzi~~ monsters
lurked in the shadows.

TEXTS I DID NOT SEE

October 31, 11:10 p.m.

Papi: Pitit mwen, my little one, how I miss you. Please return to us.

November 1, 12:01 a.m.

Ma: WE WON'T GIVE UP ON YOU. WE LOVE YOU, DENNY.

LONG AFTER

sun turned to moon,
sky filled with stars,
vocals laid over
thumping beats,
Marissa headed to sleep
and Meat finally off the clock,
which left me
                and Merc
                        and that duffel bag on the floor
in the studio . . .

a
l
o
n
e.

                    "Let me hit the head
                    before we call it a night,"
                    Merc said.

He walked down the hall
and that bag,

half zipped open,
and for a moment
I wondered . . .

            Was the video of me and Queen Yeli in there?
            And if it was, maybe I could send it to Dali,
            with a love note, maybe even a new song.
            Would it be enough to bring her back?

The duffel bag was filled with VHS-C tapes,
but no camcorder.

I quietly ran my fingers across them,
sloppily tossed around the bag,
no organization whatsoever.

Each was labeled with a name
the first was Marissa
the rest were some names I didn't recognize.
Until I saw two
at the bottom of the pile:

Dalisay
Denver

I was sure
those were all
the homemade tapes he'd made,
over the years of working with different singers.

Studio sessions,
life on the road,
clubbing,
all the good times
on repeat.

I could send her ours,
a peace offering of sorts,
a reminder that it wasn't all bad here
when we were together.

I looked around the studio
for a VCR and saw nothing
that remotely looked like one.

I was sure he had one at least,
somewhere in that
castle of a home.

I was also sure he wouldn't miss
the two tapes, if I borrowed them
for a little while.
I just wanted to see Dali again,
even if it was through the screen.

I tossed the tapes in my AliExpress bag.
The bathroom door clicked open,
and I Supermanned it to the couch
hella quick,
put on my best show.

Merc dried his hands
on his tee,
stopped short,
looked at his bag
and then back at me,

dozing-dozing-dozing,
and then he shrugged.

"Somebody's tired," he whispered.
"Come on, let's get you to bed."

I yawned
and stretched
my arms like wings.

Merc grabbed his duffel bag,
swung it around his shoulder,
then grabbed mine, too.

And that right there
pressed fast forward
on my whole universe,
mind racing
dontopenit
dontopenit

He walked me to my
bedroom door, those tapes
hidden in my backpack
pressed against his back.

"Good night," Merc said, walking away,
"Oh, almost forgot to give you this."

He handed me my backpack
and closed the door softly behind him,
as I clutched it to my chest,
exhaling,
finally.

Those tapes weren't
the first thing I stole from Merc.
Something told me they wouldn't be my last.

A RANDOM CONFESSION:

At night
when I lay in bed,
next to Chance,
I pretended it was Dali,
which I knew was stupid
given the way she played me,
but it was enough to
chase away the lonelies.

Another random confession:

In the big brick house
on Pristine Road,
there lived a girl
in a big black room
with a loose floorboard.
The perfect hiding place
for bags of plantain chips
stolen from the pantry
(because celery dinners were boring AF),
a police officer's contact card,
a SanDisk with my song I ~~stole~~ downloaded,
and
two tiny VHS-C tapes.

TheBuzz* Follow
Buzz STAFF: Bella D! @belladblock_

CONCERT CANCELED AMID ALLEGATIONS

Crossover R&B star Sean "Mercury" Ellis was scheduled to perform at Pepperdine University this Saturday; however, after a petition from students and faculty, the Los Angeles school has decided to cancel the concert. Link in bio for more details.

Liked by IamJessie and 298,512 others

View all 7,703 comments

GwennieLafleur: My sister @denverlee01 went missing after @kingmerc kidnapped her. Denny, if you can see this, PLEASE reach out to your family! We went to the @kingmerc Detroit concert to find you. His squad shut us down. We are #hurting so bad sis.

Damnboi23: Dumb move Pepperdine. Nobody turns down the KING!

GoneFlying: @gwennielafleur I just saw her w Merc @HaloLounge downtown Atlanta. She ain't missing. She just don't miss YO ASS! #drama

MommaBear: @gwennielafleur can you DM me? My daughter @IsabelFaddenBae went to Merc's concert in Detroit too and never came home. I called the cops, the news, no one cares cuz #BlackGirlsDontMatter

WeStillMatterOrg: DM for details on the next #MuteMerc protest, coming to a city near you.

I NEVER SAW

that post on Instagram,
never saw the comments,
only heard the aftermath
of Marissa telling Merc
about the concert being
canceled.
And I thought:

Mannnnn . . .
cancel culture was
alive and well!

Dumb folks
sure loved
getting
trapped

    By rumors
    By hearsay
    By lies
    By FAKE NEWS!

                Canceled shows meant

hours-long meetings
in the studio,
with lawyers,
executives,
every single important
#TeamMerc decision maker.

            An epic scramble to
        clean up traces of dirt,
         the residue of lies
           spread online.

And for me,
hours spent in the
great big black room
on Pristine Road,
where Merc said I had to stay,
only to leave for dog walks and meals.

Nothing but time to kill,
guitar on my lap,
song book at my side,
lyrics took over . . .

I'LL RISE

Written by Denver Lafleur

Verse:

There was a time I was down
and no one else was around
but you . . . you knew
just what to do
to make me feel that

Chorus:

I'll rise
(with you here by my side)

I'll soar
(your love, it makes me fly)

I'll touch
(the stars and the sun)

I'll reach
(all the way to #1)

Everything I could dream,
it's because you love me.
So, I'll rise.

THIS WAS MERC'S GAME PLAN FOR DAMAGE CONTROL

1. A pre-Thanksgiving concert (right in his old 'hood)
2. Free tickets, free food
3. A brand-new show

Bags packed
      First-class plane tickets purchased
            Georgia to California
                  Operation #MuteTheHaters was in full effect!

(just before dawn)

It all happened so fast,
I thought I was dreaming.
The swish of the door,
the tap-tap of Chance's nails on the floor,
bolting down the steps, happily breaking free.

> I didn't feel her hands
> wrapped around my shoulders.
> It was the tearing of skin
> from manicured nails
> that blasted me awake.

Black eyes,
red hair,
illuminated by a silver moon.

> "Where is it?" Marissa whispered.

"Where's what?" I asked, voice yawn-coated.

> "You took something from Merc."

Lights flicked on,
Marissa began pacing my room.
clothes, hangers,
books, drawers
tossed like mad.

> I kept my eyes on her,
> refused to look at the floor . . .
> that hidden wooden cave,
> keeper of chips, a business card,
> and two tapes I'd never fess up to stealing.

"Maybe you're the one
who took something from him."
My words, a threat,
slowed the movement of her steps.
And then she got all up in my face.

> "I told Merc he's too trusting, that he needs
> cameras all through this house. You're lucky
> he's afraid of his shit being hacked, otherwise
> I'd have you on tape with your little sticky-finger
> ass! Never understood him bringing you and
> your little lover girl up in here anyway."

319

Just before storming off,
Marissa hit me with one final blow.

"Clean this shit up!"

Then she slammed that door,
and I begged my whole body
to stop trembling.

That night, I was sure of three things:

1. There was no surveillance in that house whatsoever.
2. There was something on those tapes that I wasn't supposed to see.
3. Marissa ain't trust me. Not even a little. And if she wasn't watching me before, homegirl was about to start. For real for real.

WEIGHT: 30.6 LBS DOWN

Breakfast: nothing
Lunch: nothing
Dinner: See above
Snack: 71 plantain chips

The human body is
a confounding thing.

We feed it,
stretch bellies,
skin,
limbs
to the limit.

The body splits itself
in two.

The before
and
The after

The before was for me;
an imperfectly sculpted
shell of who I chose to be.

The after,
that is for him,
or I guess,
them.

The world that is filled
with sweet melodies,
whispering in your ear:

Perfection is near.
Keep going.

                        Seemed like all of Crenshaw
        showed up for the free
holiday meal
and of course
to see
the King of R&B
unplugged,
talent
unmatched.

Vocals stripped
down to just him
and the music.

No booty-twerking
backup dancers.
No Sharmaine,
no Althea,
no *me*.

I stood
by the
backstage curtains
and watched that man
rip and belt
through acoustic versions
of his hit songs

until he reached
the end of the set.

"My last song is an exclusive.
Singing it for the first time . . .
wrote it just for y'all. It's called 'I'll Rise.'"

Then he had the nerve to look at me . . .
and wink.

Heartbeat ripped through my chest,
every lyric
ripped from the pages of
MY BOOK
from
MY ROOM

poured from his mouth

leaving me feeling
robbed,
touched,
naked.

Made me wonder . . .
What else did he take from me?

I pictured myself running onto that stage,
grabbing that guitar,
that mic,
and giving the song its rightful home.

Because I never gave it to him.
Never even sang the melody for him.
He took my words,
flipped it
slipped it
dipped in . . .

        But I'm frozen in place
        because much as I hate it
        what he's done with the song is . . .
              genius.

But he built that genius on something
that wasn't his to take.

           The crowd applauded
        like thunder
at Sunday church service.

Lights flashed
People chanted

Merc!
Merc!
Merc!

Screaming,
begging
him to sing
that song,
my song,
one more time.

And I just stood there,
like a dumbass,
watching him

swallow up my shine.
                    In the dressing room,
                              just us,
      away from the lights and the crowd,
my mouth became a torch.

Accusations,
rapid fire,
heat building up

"How could you do that, Merc?
I shoulda been up there
singing my own lyrics,
getting my shine,
my credit
as a SOLO artist."

Hands gripped on shoulders,
Merc slammed my back against the wall
over and over and over . . .
"You got a lot of nerve, Denver!"

My breath came out fast and hard,
skin on my back
tingled, puffed,
red-black-blue
slowly building

I stared into his eyes
counting veins
weaving through
blackened pupils.

Like a monster.
Is that who he truly was?

Papi, you woulda been so proud of me.
Ma, too.
Cuz I slapped him right in his face.

Merc inhaled so loud
I thought he might swallow me whole.

I cried,
one burning tear,
splashing right on his hand,
gripped around my arm.

            Something about that seized him,

woke him up,
the monster slowly fading,
left me wondering
if when
he'd be back.

Merc served up his apology
with a side of grown-man tears.
"I wanted to surprise you, baby gurl."

Pulled me in close
held me tight
a fatherly touch
I didn't realize I needed.

Tears leaked rapid pace
my mind swirled with hunger
and loss
and longing
for the familiar. Dali, Family, Home.

"I'm so sorry I got angry with you."

Merc poured on all the reasons:

grueling schedule,
big things on the horizon,
lack of sleep,
fighting the haters
tryna bring a brotha down.
"I promise I'll make it up to you."
And he did.
Merc went outta his way:

gifts on Thanksgiving,
nights out on the town,
that track recorded with MY name as cowriter,
plus it turns out
the whole song mix-up was my fault
—left my lyrics in the kitchen by accident one day—
Merc thought it was a gift . . . from me to him—
not like he copped it from my personal space.

Was it all enough
to make me stay?

The bruises on my back
said one thing,
but then $25,000
said something else.

25 g's secured in a trust fund,
money that, according to Merc,
I'd made for writing "I'll Rise."

    The same song that
    a week after performing,
    blazed the radio airwaves.
    The more the song played,
    the bigger that number would get.

25 g's wasn't enough
to break away,
step into my own spotlight.
Not yet, at least.

  Still! I had an instant #1 hit! A future record with Queen Yeli on deck!

    I wanted to shout all the way to Shohola
    so that you and Ma would know
    I was making moves . . . and I'd be just fine. See?

ONCE UPON A BROOKLYN,

I thought I understood
the meaning of love.

Until I got to Atlanta
and learned that
love sometimes equaled

rules
and
pills
and
bruises
and
memory loss
and hunger
both
literal
and metaphorical
and
gifts
and
promises

andandandand . . .

The type of love
where when I looked
at the image in the mirror,
I barely recognized
the me I
allowed myself to *become*.

Yet, still
hidden beneath
Denver2.0
pianissimo notes
so, so soft
brewed within,
singing almost hauntingly . . .

Wake up, girl . . .
And every morning,
it was Chance who woke me up,
licking,
panting,
scratching at
walls,

vents,
doors,
really anything
to feed his curiosity.

And as silly as it sounds
to be inspired by a dog,
something about him
resonated with me.

I decided to be more like Chance.
Light a torch beneath questions
simmering within . . .

about this whole
situation I put myself in.
It was time to dig.

BlackHollywoodReporter* Follow
BHR STAFF: Alex Rodriguez @AnotherARod

SEAN "MERCURY" ELLIS LANDS LEAD ROLE IN BIOPIC

The King of R&B is ready to flex his acting muscles! According to Entertainment Weekly, the "I'll Rise" chart topper has signed with Warner Brothers for a biopic of the legendary soul singer Marvin Gaye. Filming in Atlanta begins early December, followed by shoots in Los Angeles and DC. Read up on the latest. Link in bio!

Liked by RealQueenYeli and 512,049 others

View all 12,962 comments

Simm0625: Look at God! You get'em Merc!

Rissa914: When they go low, we go high. #BlackBoyMagic

Honeypie: That's my dude right there!

LeeLeex: SMH! Marvin Gaye is turning in his grave right now!

1:21 a.m.

Sometimes when I slept

I heard
an endless stream of
different voices.

A cry here,
a scream there.

That night, it woke me up
and I saw Chance
scratching at the air vent,
his little voice letting out
the saddest whimper.
"What's wrong, my pup?"

The noises I dreamt about weren't there—
maybe it was Chance crying
but he was still scratching
like he was looking for something.

Or . . .
maybe I needed to take lil' man
outside to handle his business.

THREE THINGS FOLKS SHOULD KNOW ABOUT OTTERHOUNDS:

1. Squirrels are equal parts friend and food.
2. Open fields are too hard to resist.
3. And so are holes in chain-link fences.

I should have probably
thanked Ahmed
for the supreme running stamina
'cause my feet flew fast enough
to chase Chance
past the peach trees
all the way to that glorious
hole in the back fence.

I threw my arms around his body,
right before he sprinted through.

And thank God,
because behind that fence was
something that was missing
from the front of Merc's house:

an actual road
with moving cars,
streetlights,
civilization!

Hands gripped tight
on Chance's leash,
we walked through the grass,
past the pool house,
a crack of the front door
stopping me in my tracks.

"Can I get something to eat now?"
a voice whispered.

I whipped around hella fast,
almost tangling myself
in the leash.

Two eyes pierced the darkness.

"Who are you?"

Silence.

"What's your name?"

"Nobody."

Then "Nobody" closed the door.
                              "HEY! Open up!"
Heartbeat quickening,
I twisted
and pulled
on that knob,
open-hand-slapped
the door on repeat,

the sound of each slam
echoing all around the yard.

Inside the main house, the kitchen light
flicked on
and Merc swiftly emerged
into the dark.

                    "Yo, Denver, what's the problem?"
Anxiety on 100,
words poured like lava.

"There's someone in there!
Who is that, Merc?
Why is she asking for food?"

                    "My cousin Natasha,"
                    Merc cut me off midflow.
                    "She's visiting from New York."

"Why wouldn't she come out?"

                    "Somebody's extra nosy tonight.
                    She's sick. Probably thought you were the maid
                    bringing her soup."

Here's the thing.
The maid was gone for the night.
And that girl didn't sound sick.
She sounded . . . *lost.*

                    "Get back to bed, Denver."
                    He stepped forward, I stepped back.
"But . . ."

                    Warm hand laced into the coldness of mine,
                    voice changed from stone to honey.
                    "Come on, baby gurl."
Merc walked Chance and me
back to my room,
but sleep was the last thing on my mind.

Eyes wide open,
I had a dream that night.
I stood on a mountaintop,
eyes scanning the clouds.

In the distance,
beyond green meadows,
rushing rivers,
and sky-kissing castles,

a beautiful sculpture of a man
clenched his fists,
limbs, muscles, veins
transforming from human
to green-skinned dragon.

In the moon-crescent of his eyes,
the target of his hunger . . .
me.

Wings spread wide,
he flew above the clouds,
licked his fangs at the sight of me
standing mountain-tall,
fire gathered, belly-to-throat

I drew my arrow,
steel-coated,
lightning fast
and let it soar,

the arrow lodging in its left eye,
the fire-breathing dragon,
went tumbling
down.

And I tell you, Papi,
it was the realest
fucking nightmare
I ever conjured up.

MONDAY, DECEMBER 9

Merc's new movie role
meant my time in the studio
went from seven days a week
to negative zero point nothing.
Then one night . . .

> "Wanna watch some Marvin Gaye
> classics with me, baby gurl?
> Help me get into character before I head to set?"

Merc, standing in my doorway,
for the first time in days.

Took me a second
to realize that a classic
Marvin Gaye performance
just might be
played on a VCR.

"Sure, Merc.
I'd love to."

of the great big house
on Pristine Road,
there was a room
I never knew existed.

"Whoa!" My eyes bugged out as we walked in.
"This place is magical, Merc."

The Galaxy Room
built of wood, painted black,
a constellation of stars
drawn on the ceiling

comfy oversized couches
fluffy pillows everywhere,
a big movie screen,
and behold . . .
a VCR!

I wouldn't have even known
had I not seen Merc
open the doors to a
large, mirrored wall unit,

inside revealing
an entire library of
1980s classics like
Ghostbusters,
The Goonies,
and *Coming to America*.

And next to that,
a Panasonic PV-4661 VCR.

We sat on the floor together.
As he showed off his ancient pride and joy,
I ran my fingers across Merc's collection.

"Do you use these to record
on your camcorder?" I asked innocently.

"Nah, baby gurl. My films are VHS
tapes. My personal recordings are done
on VHS-C."

He proudly held up two tapes

showing me the difference.

> "For this little one, you need an adapter
> to watch it." He rummaged through the wall unit,
> and then held it up. "See, like this."

He placed the small VHS-C
into the large adapter
and like magic
the video could play in the VCR.

Then he put the adapter back in the wall unit,
my eyes taking note of exactly where

bottom drawer to the left
> "Let's get started, shall we? I'ma
> introduce you to *my* King of R&B!
> You ready?"

I nodded fiercely.

Merc pulled a tape from his collection:
Marvin Gaye Live in Belgium, 1981
and slipped it in the VCR.

Then he walked around the room,
drawing the blinds,
shutting off the lights.

On the great big screen,
grainy images
sprang to life,

a singer turned actor
studied Marvin Gaye's every move,
repeating lyric for lyric,
line by line
while the girl
with eyes of fading starlight,
watched the musical genius from the floor.

Just when the credits rolled,
there was a bang at the door.
Marissa stuck her head in.

"Time to go . . . Merrrc . . ."
Marissa held out his name
extra long soon as she saw me.

Homegirl was all done up

in a little black dress,
material so shiny,
looked like she took it
straight out the Hefty box.

"Don't you look nice!" I lied,
but Marissa rolled her eyes.

"Baby gurl, thanks for the movie date.
We'll do it again real soon."
Merc hugged me.

That one touch
birthed thorns on my skin.

"Tell Meat to bring the car around."
Merc zipped his leather coat.

"Meat should stay here . . . with Denver."
Code for: Marissa didn't trust my ass one bit.

I could see Merc consider it for a second,
until I squeezed his wrist and said,
"I'm tired, bro. I'll just go to bed."

Merc clapped his hands.
"See? That's my baby gurl. Let's roll."

Then him and Marissa and that *face*
booked it outta there.

Once I was clear they'd left
the grounds,
I raced to my room,
lifted the loose floorboard,
two VHS-C tapes clutched
beneath my robe,
Chance trailing behind.

I flew through the dark,
empty house,
past the dining room,
past the kitchen,
through the hall
lined with bookshelves,
until Chance stopped
and began sniffing and licking books.
"That's not food, silly!"

I grabbed him by the collar
and hightailed it back
to the Galaxy Room.

Whipped open the door,
that old-school VCR staring me down . . .
Let's do this.

I popped
the tape labeled *Dalisay* in.
The screen, fuzzy at first,
followed by a clearer,
yet shaky image.

Dali danced seductively
and I figured it was an act,
maybe something
we would've used in the show,
until the screen faded to black
and a new image poured in.

Dali . . . *my* Dali on her knees,
pink cheeks,
fresh tears,
lips quivering,
video revealing
the fullness of her
and the bottom half
of a man
as he unbuckled his belt,
yanked Dali's chin toward ~~him~~ *it*,
and she opened her mouth
W I D E.

> Hands cupping my whole face,
> I couldn't look
> I couldn't look
> Anymore.

What was he doing?
Why didn't Dali tell me?
Who was that guy?
It wasn't Merc.
It couldn't be.
He would never . . .
ever . . .
Right? RIGHT?

I looked at the screen

again.
It was then
that I noticed
her outfit . . .
the same one
from the concert,
the night we first met . . .
Merc.

I yanked that tape—*HIS* tape—
out so fast
wanting to light a fire,
toss it to the flames.

                                        Blood
                              turned to ice
                              turned to heat
                              turned to rage
                              turned to fear

I needed to talk to someone
and not Merc
and then I remembered . . .

the day after Dali left
he unlocked my phone features
with a special code
But then he changed it again.

I thought of the first code,
asked myself why was it so special

0-2-2-7
0-2-2-7
Wasn't that when . . .

he won his first Grammy?
February 27

So what other dates would
mean just as much to him?

                              Fingers trembled
                                through several
                        four-digit combinations,
                          getting them all wrong,

until my brain,
like a camera,

flashed a memory,
June 14, the day we first met.

Could that be special to him?
0-6-1-4

And just like that,
the home page
flashed into view.

Fingers held steady
as I dialed

One ring . . .
>*The number you have reached is disconnected.*
>*Please hang up and try again.*

Next number.
It rang . . .
and rang . . .
and rang . . .
And then . . .
"Hello?"

                          "Shak, it's me."
"Denver?"
Shak screamed in F sharp,
and I shushed her fast.
                    "Where's Dali?" I asked.
"Denver, are you . . . *crying*?"
                    "I just need to get ahold of Dali." I sniffed back tears.
"Why you asking me?"
                    "Well, don't you see her at school?"

"School? Dali doesn't go to school.
Aren't you guys on tour?"

                    "Shak?"
"Yeah."
                    "Dali went home two months ago."

"Denver?
Nobody's seen her around here
since the day y'all left . . ."

THIS WAS THE PART WHERE

                                                    I called the police, Papi.

                    This was the part where
                    flashes of light
                    red-white-blue,

              broke through
              iron gates,
              chain-link fences,
              and rescued

        the stupid girl
        with stars for eyes,

        drove past
        Georgia peach trees,
        snaked through
        snowcapped Pocono Mountains,
        until they took her
        all the way
                        home

        to Ma
        and Gwen
        and *you*.

                              Except

        this is the part where
        that didn't happen.

        Because I needed to find Dali.
        And I needed to know something else.
        If she didn't tell me about this,
        what else did she keep from me?

CHANCE LAFLEUR:

<pre>
                              expert licker
                            master barker
                            bionic listener
                          of faraway sounds
                          I could not detect
</pre>

His groan, a low, slow boil,
as I began to switch
from Dali's tape to my own,
but then it came in hot, rolling, fast

<pre>
                      Chance scratched at my knees,
                        then ran to the window
                          facing the driveway,
                        and clawed at the glass.
</pre>

Somebody was coming home
and we needed to haul ass . . .
FAST!

Both tapes lodged beneath my arms,
cell phone tucked in my pocket,

feet zipped through halls,
past bookshelves,
kitchen-dining-living room(s)
—car door slammed—

<pre>
                          up up up
                      I skipped steps,
                    two, three at a time,
                  Chance hot on my trail
</pre>

phone on my nightstand,
tapes hidden beneath wooden floor,
foyer doors opened below,
buried myself deep
under thick covers.

Me and Chance taking turns panting
as hard shoes click-clacked
up up up wooden steps.

I smelled the scent of her
—lilacs and trouble—
before I saw the shadow
of her heels beneath the door.
Hovering . . . listening . . .

as I begged my lips to remain muted.

This is the call she thought
I didn't hear

"Meat, yeah, it's me, Marissa.
Listen, I'm gonna need you
to beef up security around here.

I'll get extra detail on Merc.
But I need you based here . . .
to keep an eye on things."

I should have left,
I could have left,
I *would* have left

But Dali.

And there was this other thing,
this feeling burrowed deep inside.

Spent my whole life
being made to feel like I wasn't
smart enough
good enough
doing enough

But there in that moment
I KNEW exactly who I was
      fearless
           gifted
                 brilliant . . .

Way smarter than Merc
for all his fake-ass genius
and money
and power.
I had those tapes, didn't I?

And I was smart enough
to figure a way to make his ass
pay for what he did
to my best friend.

That night,
in the great big house
on Pristine Road,
I prayed that God
would transform me into a spider.

Black body,
hard shell,
belly brimming
toxic secrets,
spinning silken threads
plunging
fearlessly,
noiselessly
into a web of truths
waiting to be revealed.

Meat aka glorified babysitter
on active double duty.
—Marissa's request—

But I caught that man
beginning to slip a long time ago.

Starting with that song
he allowed me to
~~steal~~ download
when Merc wasn't around,

And those nights where
even though I know he was told to,
he "forgot" to lock my bedroom door

A soft teddy bear of a man,
hardened exterior unraveling
with my every joke,
my every pouty request

And lately,
always on his phone, texting,
Snapchatting for hours
while Merc and Marissa
stayed on set.

"You must got a girlfriend or something?" I asked.

The blush of Meat's cheeks,
a gentle plunge into my web.

Nancy Dixon,
thighs thick enough
to make grown men cry,
worked in downtown Atlanta
at Babette's Café.

They had been kickin' it
for a hot minute,
but extra hours on the job
meant less hours for her.

"She's mad cuz
it's the third time
this week I bailed on her.

And I'm tripping, too.
I can barely do my job right.
Shortie got me falling hard."

"You should go," I said, coughing.
"I don't feel too good, so I'm going to sleep."

                    "Nah. Merc'll kill me if I leave you here alone.
                    I'll get up with Nancy another day."
"I won't tell."

                    "Denver, don't do that blinky, cutesy eye thing!"

My web grew longer, stronger.

". . . orrrr you can keep letting her down
but don't be mad when she dumps you."

                    "Fine. You win. Just don't say nuthin!"

SOMETIMES

the
threat
of
losing
is
enough
to
bring
anyone
to
their
knees.

SOON AS I HEARD TIRES ROLL,

I grabbed my shit
from the floorboards,
couldn't get to the
Galaxy Room fast enough,
Chance racing ahead of me.

I slipped the tape with my name
in the adapter and
then the VCR and pressed
PLAY.
It was a video of our
first night clubbing with Merc.
We were dancing, drinking,
but then the image cut into a new one.

Location:
Hitmaker Studio in New York,
the one with the bed
and the doors
and the lights
and the blood.

My naked body,
eyes closed,
legs wide open,
mouth on mute,
one arm dangling,
and the monster unfurling,
growling on top of me.

AND

I

   broke

      and

         broke

           and

              broke

                into

                  a

                    thousand

                        tiny

S
H
A
T
T
E
R
E
D

pieces.

I FELT WHATEVER

was left
inside me
S
N
A
P

Crying
screaming
longing to break something
break HIM

But it would've
nevereverever been
enough.

                    Everything became clear:
                that pain I'd felt the next day,
                     the blood after,
              feeling split to bits, inside out.

My skin no longer
felt like my own.

I wanted to rip myself
out of myself
leaving behind
the touched,
torched,
humiliated
shards
of me.

                        Eyes burning with tears,
                              rage,
                    terror like I'd never known

I had to get out of there
Me and Chance and
. . .
he wasn't there.
Someone else was.

Quiet   servant
frozen   shadow

I
never
ever
learned
her
name

mouth   gaped
eyes   wide

At the image
still playing on the screen
A montage of guy-on-girl

Planet Mercury,
all 800 degrees
of fiery surface,

incinerating
what lay beneath to ash

"I'm so sorry!" she stuttered,
"Please don't tell Merc!"

And then she ran away so fast
I didn't get a chance
to beg the same of her.

I PRESSED

STOP,

grabbed that tape,
ran through the halls,
mind spinning I-am-not-safe-I-am-not-safe,
tears gushing fast and furious,
until I found Chance scratching
at that bookshelf again.

This time, so hard
a few books fell to the floor.

I put them back,
every limb trembling,
pressed too hard, I guess,
because the shelf
click-clicked

and the
whole wall
opened like a door

and that's when I saw . . .
stairs.

CHANCE

darted into the pit of darkness
sniffing and whimpering
every step of the way

And I
ran-and-ran-and-ran
sobbing through panted breaths

A long, winding maze
two walls lined with doors
three to each side.

Chance stopped at the first one
started scratching at it like mad.

That's when I heard a voice:
"Who's there?"

IN THE BIG BRICK HOUSE

on Pristine Road
there lay a hidden maze,
its winding halls
padded with silence,
ceiling to floor,
six doors, equidistant,
each one complete
with a tiny covered window.

If you lifted the first one,
you would see a girl on a bed,
tucked in the corner,
hands clutched on swollen belly

And the second you did,
you would search frantically
for something, anything
to open that door
and break her

F
    R
       E
         E

I CRIED HYSTERICALLY

as Dali stood and ran to me,
her hands reaching through the window,
the warmth of her touch
not enough to keep me from
trying to rip that door off

"I'm so sorry!
I'm so sorry!"

We finished each other's words

I	didn't
know	he
did	that
to	you

. . .

us

But that chorus set me off even more
"THIS IS MY FAULT!" I cried.

"I thought if I just did
what Merc wanted, we'd get famous faster.
I didn't think he would hurt you, too.
I should have said something, Denver."

Dali started sobbing
whole body convulsing,
sliding down the door.

I yanked and pulled,
begging the universe
for Herculean strength.

"I'm getting you out of here right now—"

Chance started barking like mad.
Was someone here?

"You gotta go back up," Dali begged.

"I can't leave you down here!"

"No one will believe us, Denver!
It's our word against his.
Plus he's got on us on Insta
saying we chose to come here."

"Dali, I've got the tapes of what he did. Evidence."

"And he is never gonna let you leave
this house with those tapes. You need
to get upstairs now, before we're both
trapped down here!"

"Okay, I'm going, but I will get you out
and I'm gonna make him pay, Dali!"

"Denver?"

"Yes?"

Dali pointed her lips down the hall.

"There are more of us.
They are everywhere.
All around
if you look close enough."

I HAULED ASS TO MY ROOM,

video evidence tucked beneath the floor,

my mind a revolving swirl of
                the girl down the hall from my room
                        the girl at the concert
                                the girl in the pool house

                the broken girl in the bed (me)

teeth sinking
deeper into bloodied lips.

All the jagged,
splintered
pieces of me
left behind in that studio in New York
without me even knowing
just how far things went

Fragments
left behind with my best friend,
in a hidden dungeon in this house,

left behind onstage
when Merc claimed what was rightfully mine

And a plan began to form in
my good-enough
smart-enough
brilliant brain

I was going to mute this
MONSTER
for good.

TUCKED IN BED,

covers over my head,
Merc cracked my door open,
walked slowly to me
and touched my hair,
that one touch
turned me to a mountain of ice.

Pretending I was sleeping,
deep breaths in and out,
he whispered in my ear

"Heard you haven't been feeling good.
I gotta film for a couple days, so I won't
see you. But Meat will be here,
on double duty. And when
I get back, I'm all yours."

He kissed my forehead,
and walked out my room
I opened my eyes
and didn't close them
for the rest of the night.

ONCE UPON A TIME,

the gray-eyed monster
kissed his prey
in the still of the night,
not knowing
that come morning,
that one kiss
would birth another monster
far more powerful,
its fangs and claws
dripping with
honey-coated venom.

1:59 a.m.

Sprawled out on the couch,
Meat slept beneath
a cold December moon,

I explored la Casa de Merc,
spider legs scuttled silently,

searching undiscovered rooms,
        hunting,
                gathering,

until my AliExpress backpack
was filled with
envelopes,
tape,
bubble wrap,
and the most precious
find of all
tucked in an office cabinet:

shiny
black
metal

fire
ready
for
angry
fingertips
at a moment's notice.

I'd never seen a gun in real life before
not in person
not even in our old 'hood
that Ma and Papi thought was unsafe

At first I couldn't
bring myself to touch it

It felt heavy
and
dead
and
cold

A bludgeon
An anchor

I had no choice
but to steal it

Figured it was safer with me
than it'd ever be with him

And I was safer with *it*
than I ever, ever was
with Sean "Mercury" Ellis.

5:21 p.m.

Pulling at the darkening skin
sagging beneath his eyes,
Meat gazed at his reflection
in the mirror above the fireplace.

Cologne freshly sprayed,
bald head, coconut-oil shining.
"Denver, I gotta bounce for like
two, three hours, or my girl's gonna kill me."

Hands clutching my belly,
a performance worthy of an Emmy,
I begged, "I need a ride to the store."

Long, drawn-out sigh. "For what?"

"Maxi pads."

"Merc's got plenty of that stuff in the—"
"We're out. I checked."

A pause.
I could see Meat's
brain percolating.

"I mean, I guess you could go
and I'll just tell Merc and—"

"Nah, he's still away. I'll just bring 'em to you.
Er, what kind?"

"Always.
With wings.
Overnight.
Lilac scented—"

"Let's just hurry up.
Bout to make a brotha late late!"

"Thanks, let me grab my backpack!"

Downtown Alpharetta was lined with
Christmas trees, and hordes of people,
street parking almost impossible to find.

"Can I have some money?" I held out my hand.

Meat shook his head.
"We got a name for folks
like you, where I come from:
Beggin' Bertha!"

He reached into his pocket and
then pulled out a twenty,
and I hoped it would be enough to do enough.

"Why don't you stop at that florist down the street?
Get your girl some calla lilies."

"Nah, I'ma wait. Walgreens is
right there,"
Meat insisted.

My stomach rumbled
tryna figure out how to
get this man OUT my face.

"I mean, I guess if that's how
you wanna roll up on shortie.
Late *and* empty-handed."

Meat eyed the distance
from the pharmacy to the florist.
Close, but not close enough to walk.
"What you say again? Calla lilies?"

I hit him with a nod,
slammed the car door,
and exhaled loud as hell,
as he busted a U-turn in the middle of
Main Street.

to zip in and out
of that post office
next to Walgreens.

Heart pounded,
waiting in a line,
that seemed ten
minutes too long,
I didn't have that kind of time.

I went up to one of those
speedy self-serve machines,
typed in the address,
fingers frantically
pressing
all the proper buttons
to select media mail

I didn't care that it'd
take up to ten days
to reach the destination
all that mattered was that it arrived

A hot tear sprinted
down my cheek
as I bypassed
the long line
and placed my package in the outgoing bin

"Miss, are you okay?" the clerk asked.
Could she see
my hands trembling?
Hear the mezzo forte
of my beating heart?
"I'm fine." I wiped my face,

and hauled ass to the pharmacy,
grabbed the cheapest pads
I could find,
self-checkout to hurry the process.

And just as I walked out
the store,
I bumped into Meat
holding a beautiful bouquet

of calla lilies.
                    "How'd I do?" He beamed.

"Not bad, lover boy."
I slapped his shoulder,
walking back to the car.

"Ay yo, where's my change, Denver?"

"Change?" I smirked
as I opened the door.
"Man, you really don't know much
about women, do you?
Here's your quarter."

I SMILED THE WHOLE RIDE HOME

because
despite all the pain
brewing within,
I found a gift . . .
a reason to smile that night.

Meat pulled up to the front steps,
put the car in park,
to let me out.

"Hey, Denver." He rolled down the window.
"I know this music thing is taking a toll on you.
On the real, I think you can do better
than Merc. Be *bigger* than him.
But you ain't hear that from me.
Try and feel better, okay?"

And for a second,
I almost felt bad
for lying to him.
Almost.
        "That's the plan,"
        I replied.

And then Meat and his gentle smile
and those flowers
pulled off beneath a darkening sky.

I took one last look
at that mansion,
and whispered to the cold wind,
"I did it, Dali. *We* did it."

SOON AS I GOT THROUGH

the front door,
my feet hit the floor running.

I unlocked my phone,
having memorized a series of
codes
Merc changes at will

Fingers scrambled through combinations
till I landed on the most obvious of all
1-2-2-9
his birthday

Home page sprang to life
I couldn't dial fast enough

                            She picked up
                on the first ring.
"Ma?"

"DENVER?"
Sobbing and screaming became one.

"I don't have much time.
I just called to say I'm sorry
and
I love you
and
I'm coming home—

"Both me and Dali . . .
Tonight."

IT'S LIKE

there was a button
inside me
and someone
clicked ON

I flew down the hall,
backpack strapped
to my shoulders

Pushed on the bookshelf
hard, not caring if
I broke it

Jumped over steps,
two, three at a time
until I reached Dali's door,
lifted the small window and saw . . .
no one.

EVERY

single

door

empty.

MOUTH,
dry.
Hands,
wet.
Feet,
RUN!

UP   UP   UP   the steps!

panic   rising

time   ticking
. . .   . . .

"LOOKING FOR SOMETHING?"

I heard the monster's voice
before I saw
his shadow.

                              My vocal cords
              exploded.

"I know what you are," I spat at his face,
"and I know what you did to me.
You're a fucking MONSTER!
Now tell me where Dali is
before I call the cops!"

But he was fast.
Too fast.

Two gloved hands
wrapped tight
around my neck
the weight of them
crushing my instrument
slowly.

But free hands
turned to Brooklyn fists
slamming hard against
Merc's eyes,
mouth,
nose,
knees-to-nuts,
the final blow.

Chance barked wildly,
darted down the steps,
jumped on his hind legs,
smiling, licking both of us
like it was a goddamned party.

I grabbed a vase
launched it straight at Merc's head,
heard him wince and fall to his knees

I hauled ass out the kitchen doors,
Chance right on my tail,
past the patio,
past the peach trees,

eyes scanning the darkness
for that broken,
open chain-link fence.

But I was the only one focused
because Chance saw a squirrel
and zipped off in a different direction

      There was no time
      to grab him

Not when
I realized
Merc was chasing me

Just a few feet more,
I begged my feet to move faster

Because once I got through
that hole,
I was gonna flag down
the first car I saw.

But I heard him closer,
the pounding of his steps
drawing near,

I took one look behind me
and just like the white girls
in the horror movies
what did my Black ass do?

   F

      A

         L

           L

                           Merc
                 pounced on top of me
             and started screaming,
        "Bitch, you trying to ruin me?
      After everything I did for you?"

That voice echoed up to the clouds

slapping   kicking
punching   rolling

My backpack ripped open,
black metal rolling out,

reflecting
beneath starry skies . . .

       Some monsters were made of
       storms and fire,
with hands
fast enough
to wrap
fingers around
triggers and

   P

      U

        L

          L.

A single shot
through my gut
          muted *Merc*
          but didn't end me.
      Yet.

Earth's rotation on pause,
a staggered sip of breath
the gun unreachable
in the grass

But it was fine,
because I won,
no matter what
the universe chose for me next.

The world would know
that Sean "Mercury" Ellis is a predator.

That he hurt Dalisay Gómez
and Denver Lee Lafleur
and God knows how many more?

I didn't let him get away with it
because my voice STILL mattered
even though he tried
to take it away from me.

EYES FLUTTERING,

ever-so-slowly,
I saw Marissa
dart through tree-lined fields,
moonlight haloing fiery hair,

as Merc towered above me,
sobbing wordlessly as I bled and bled
O
U
T
I heard the panting of her breath,
the desperation in her voice.
"What did you do, Merc?"
                        "Denver found . . . She was gonna . . ."

"Don't say another word!
You can't be here!
I told you not to trust this one.
Get back to set. I'll take care of this."

I saw Marissa's gloved hands
wipe down the gun,
collect the shell off the ground.

Run back inside the house
crash expensive vases,
statues, glasses
against Brazilian cherry floors.

Paint the picture
of a crime
of epic proportions.
(Just not the one that actually happened.)

Grab her phone,
dial three digits,
"I'd like to report a robbery,"
voice faux-coated with tears,

while I lay there
frozen still in the grass:
cells, muscles, organs,
dying-dying-dying.
                        I WAS COLD, Papi.
But only for a moment.

Then . . .

I WAS WARM
I WAS TIRED
I WAS ALONE
I was fading

(s
    l
        o
            w
                l
                    y)

RED LIGHT

white light,
blue light

I recognized Officer Parsons
from the night of the wellness check.

Could he hear my words,
muted behind sealed lips,
closed eyes, halted breath?

Follow the hole in the fence.
That's where Merc went.
But he didn't hear.
No one did.

I tried to hang on, Papi,
and wait for you.

Even after they tossed me
on the gurney,
drove me godknowswhere

Even after your
emergency flight
Pennsylvania to Georgia,
fast as wings could fly . . . it was too late.
Uber ride
zipped down I-85
even when your feet reached
the cold, sterile room,

where coroners drew curtains back,
your hands pounding
against Plexiglas

> the wailing
> the sobbing
> the identifying
> that that body was
> *me*.

The Earth tilted
slowly on its axis
as you signed on the dotted line,

giving examiners
permission to
poke me,
prod me,
open me,
fill me up,
drain me,
OUT

and sew the broken pieces
back together again.

Until all that was left
was a
lifeless
breathless
shell.

WEIGHT:

Does   it
even   matter
                              any   more?

                              I am weightless now.
                              Can't you see?
                              Look how the universe holds
                                                                        me.

have waited a little longer . . .
     I had so much to tell you
like . . .
     these were the things money could buy:

alibis,
  covered-up lies,
    friends in high places,
      the silence of Black and Brown girls
      looking for a come-up, a payday
        a way in . . .
          (and a way out)
And also . . .

that I messed up.
I was wrong about Merc.
Ma
and
you
and Shak
and the Browns
were right all along.

But also . . .
Y'all messed up, too.
You were wrong about ME.
I was
smart
talented
enough.

But I guess it's too late, huh?
Especially since I am here:

On this plane,
in this box.

Flying VIP
doesn't always mean
first-class seat.

Sometimes it means
boarding first on the plane
hidden away from eyes,
ears,
tears
that will surely come if passengers
see ramp agents
loading dead bodies
in bottom bunks.

41.325560° N, -74.808130° W

Final destination: Stroyan Funeral Home, Milford, PA

Will
Ma
and
Gwen
and
Tía Esme
and
Dali
and
Shak
and the Browns
and
all of Brooklyn
and
Shohola
be there
waiting for me?

Can you make sure of it, Papi?
And when we're all together again,
will you play our special song?
You know the one, right?

DECEMBER 13

EIGHTEEN-YEAR-OLD PROTÉGÉ OF SEAN "MERCURY" ELLIS SHOT DURING SUSPECTED HOME INVASION
Funeral planned post-Christmas holiday

DECEMBER 14

R&B STAR QUESTIONED IN ROBBERY/MURDER AT ATLANTA HOME
Atlanta PD confirms Ellis cleared as a suspect

DECEMBER 28

MEGA PRODUCER SEAN "MERCURY" ELLIS, SET TO CONTINUE FILMING MOVIE
R&B star back to work after mourning the death of his soon-to-debut protégé, Denver Lee Lafleur

JANUARY 3

FOUR YOUNG WOMEN, ALLEGED VICTIMS OF SEAN "MERCURY" ELLIS, DENY ACCUSATIONS OF BEING HELD CAPTIVE
Rumors surface they were paid off

Grief

There is no cure,
no magic pill,
no on or off button

It comes at will,
sits still deep within,
a keeper of sorts,

With a mind of its own
it tells *you* how long to stay,
three months in this case,
surrounded by
mountains
    and
          tears
              and
                    family

and

H
O
M
E.

But it will also
tell you when to let go,
move on,

A silent, gentle whisper
that reminds you (Gwen)
of the gift that had been waiting
all along . . .

DECEMBER 12

Gwendolyn Lafleur, R.A.
Dartmouth College
1256 Hinman
Hanover, New Hampshire 03755

Dear Gwen,
I can already FEEL you side-eyeing me!

I'm sure I'm gonna spend a long time paying for the worry I put you, Ma, and Papi through.

But I did get to live out some part of my dream at least. And I'm nowhere near done.

Merc tried to break me. Tried to take away my talent, my voice, my music. But what I'm gonna take from him will be far worse.

That's why I need you to hold on to this package for me. Please don't tell Ma and Papi. I'll explain everything when I get there. You got me, right? Last time. Promise.

See you soon,
Denny

APRIL 6

MURDER INVESTIGATION INTO THE DEATH OF DENVER
LEE LAFLEUR REOPENED AFTER DAMNING VIDEO
EVIDENCE SENT TO ATLANTA PD

APRIL 7

R&B STAR SEAN "MERCURY" ELLIS ARRESTED IN HIS
HOME. MISSING GIRL DALISAY GÓMEZ FOUND IN
BASEMENT WITH BABY.

APRIL 13

VIRAL AFTER DEATH: DISGRACED R&B STAR'S MURDER
VICTIM'S ORIGINAL SONG, "I'M THROUGH,"
DEBUTS AT #1 ON THE CHARTS

They say the greatest love stories
begin as a cliché

boy meets girl
boy and girl fall in love
and they live
happily
ever
after

But that's not how our story
~~goes~~ *went*

One day,
when
the wounds
have healed
and her ghost
subsides,

I will tell you a story,
of two girls lost in the fire,
set by
El Cuco . . .

the monster
with the fangs
and claws
and tiny hands
hidden in deep pockets,

how he cast his web
put a spell on ~~me~~ us
and weaved and weaved
until ~~I~~ we almost had nothing left.

But for now,
I gotta go.

My baby girl,
Denver Lee Gómez,
needs her mami.

ACKNOWLEDGMENTS

There's a certain relief that washes over me every time I type those magical words: *the end*.

I'm not sure I felt that this time around. I worried for the characters, for the families impacted, and more importantly, I still worry for the real-life Denvers and Dalis of the world.

So, I begin these acknowledgments by saying: I see you. In some ways, I am you. But above all, I *believe* you. And I know I'm not the only one. There's a whole village waiting to rise up and stand by your side.

On this journey of writing *Muted*, I was blessed with an incredible village of my own, who listened and guided me through the most difficult piece I've written to date.

First and foremost, giving all honor and glory to God, I thank Him for steadfastness, family, and faith.

To my endless love, Nasser Charles. We rise, we fall, but through it all, we have each other (and Sebas, of course). Thank you for protecting my peace and being my ears whenever I needed them.

Christopher Sebastian Charles, everything I do is for you. I pray that you grow into a man who will always stand up for what's right and speak out against the wrongs. I love you more than words can say.

Mom, Daddy, Tony, and Rae (so sorry I snagged your future daughter's name, but I couldn't resist!). I cherish our family bond and am eternally grateful for your love and belief in me.

To my agent-therapist, Lara Perkins. Your enthusiasm for

this book is what kept me afloat. Thank you for guiding me through some really tough moments in writing and revising *Muted*. You kept me sane and focused on what mattered most. Next book, I promise to be less dramatic!

#TeamScholastic: You sure know how to make a girl feel special! Liza Baker, thank you for making sure that *Muted* landed into the caring hands of David Levithan and Amanda Maciel.

Amanda, it's been a real joy and honor working with you on this project. You pushed me to heights I didn't think I could reach. A million thank-yous will never be enough.

Additional thanks to the other members of my Scholastic team: Ellie Berger, Talia Seidenfeld, Erin Berger, Rachel Feld, Lauren Donovan, Sydney Tillman, Elizabeth Parisi, Maeve Norton, Baily Crawford, and Melissa Schirmer. Big thanks to my talented cover artist, Adekunle Adeleke, and to model Jaycina Almond and photographer Ryan Stokes for the cover inspiration.

To my booking agent, Sarah Azibo, thank you for championing my work and taking the best care of me during my author travels.

There is no book without extra eyes to put me in check. My mother, Jennifer Carlisle-Peters, never disappoints. I can always count on you, Mom, to read my work, split my ego into teeny pieces, and put it back together again, ha! I love you.

To Sasha Baynes, I will forever be grateful to you for you coming to my house week after week during the summer of 2019 with your ink pen (lol!). You read every word, every page, start to finish, many, many times and ripped this manuscript down to the studs. You're a real one, sis!

To my word & poem count buddies, Stephanie Jones and Kelly Calabrese. Those daily check-ins (and vent sessions!) got us to the finish line. Onward!

Also, big thanks to author Kaija Langley for early reads of *Muted*. Your keen eye, particularly on Denver and Dali, meant the world to me. I pray I've done them justice.

To my family and friends who endured my endless vetting on all things Haitian and Dominican. Fallon Dumont-Sajous, Gwen Charles, Dr. Jennifer Charles, France Cortez, Amy Scott, Leslie Mondesir, Stephanie Amaro, and Kinsky Mora. Mèsi anpil! ¡Mil gracias!

A huge thank-you to the professionals who allowed me to ask questions and fact-checked so that I could give a credible depiction of what Denver and Dali experienced:

Officer Giuliana Alessandri, Elizabeth Police Department

Reginald Sconiers, former funeral director

Captain Adam Stravinsky, pilot

And finally, to my mentors for this book, two of the GOATS of this industry: Margarita Engle, 2017–2019 Young People's Poet Laureate Emeritus, and award-winning illustrator Floyd Cooper. I am honored and humbled, and I promise to pay the kindness forward.

Tami Charles is the critically acclaimed author of numerous books for young readers, including *Like Vanessa* and *Becoming Beatriz*. In her teens and early twenties, Tami enjoyed a taste of fame as a member of an all-girl R&B trio. They performed for Boyz II Men, BET, *Showtime at the Apollo*, and had a one-hit wonder on the radio. Those were the good old days! Tami's adult years would lead her to the classroom, where she worked as an educator for thirteen years before pursuing her childhood dream of becoming an author. For more information on Tami and her books, visit tamiwrites.com.